A NASTY AFFAIR

Stories

FYODOR DOSTOYEVSKY

HARPER**PERENNIAL** ● CLASSIC**STORIES**

NEW YORK ● LONDON ● TORONTO ● SYDNEY ● NEW DELHI ● AUCKLAND

HARPER**PERENNIAL** ● CLASSIC**STORIES**

FIRST HARPER PERENNIAL CLASSIC STORIES EDITION PUBLISHED 2009.

Designed by Justin Dodd

Library of Congress Cataloging-in-Publication Data is available upon request.

ISBN 978-0-06-177374-7

09 10 11 12 13 OV/RRD 10 9 8 7 6 5 4 3 2 1

A DISGRACEFUL AFFAIR

CONTENTS

WHITE NIGHTS

A Sentimental Love Story
(From the Memoirs of a Dreamer)

TRANSLATED BY DAVID MAGARSHACK

And was it his destined part
Only one moment in his life
To be close to your heart? . . .

                       —Ivan Turgenev

that the whole world would have nothing to do with me. You may ask who "the whole world" is. For, I am afraid, I have not been lucky in acquiring a single acquaintance in Petersburg during the eight years I have been living there. But what do I want acquaintances for? I know the whole of Petersburg without them, and that, indeed, was the reason why it seemed to me that the whole world had forsaken me when the whole town suddenly arose and left for the country. I was terrified to be left alone, and for three days I wandered about the town plunged into gloom and absolutely at a loss to understand what was the matter with me. Neither on Nevsky Avenue, nor in the park, nor on the embankment did I meet the old familiar faces that I used to meet in the same place and at the same time all through the year. It is true I am a complete stranger to these people, but they are not strangers to me. I know them rather intimately, in fact; I have made a very thorough study of their faces; I am happy when they are happy, and I am sad when they are overcast with care. Why, there is an old gentleman I see every day on the Fontanka Embankment with whom I have practically struck up a friendship. He looks so thoughtful and dignified, and he always mutters under his breath, waving his left hand and holding a big knotty walking-stick with a gold top in his right. I have, I believe, attracted his attention, and I should not be surprised if he took a most friendly interest in me. In fact, I am sure that if he did not meet me at a certain hour on the Fontanka Embankment he would be terribly upset. That is why we sometimes almost bow to one another, especially when we are both in a good humour. Recently we had not seen each other for two days, and on the third day, when we met, we were just about to raise our hats in salute, but fortunately we recollected days. In the street I felt out of sorts (this one had gone, that one had gone, and where on earth had the other one got to?), and at home I was not my old self, either. For two evenings I had been racking my brains trying hard to discover what was wrong with my room. What was it made me so peevish when I stayed there? And, greatly perplexed, I began examining my grimy green walls and the ceiling covered with cobwebs which Matryona was such a genius at cultivating. I went over my furniture and looked at each chair in turn, wondering whether the trouble lay there (for it upsets me to see even one chair not in its usual place); I looked at the window—but all to no purpose: it did not make me feel a bit better! I even went so far as to call in Matryona and rebuke her in a fatherly sort of way about the cobwebs and her untidiness in general. But she just gave me a surprised look and stalked out of the room without saying a word, so that the cobwebs still remain cheerfully in their old places. It was only this morning that at last I discovered the real cause of my unhappiness. Oh, so they are all running away from me to the country, are they? I'm afraid I must apologise for the use of this rather homely word, but I'm not in the mood now for the more exquisite refinements of style, for everybody in Petersburg has either left or is about to leave for the country; for every worthy gentleman of a solidly-prosperous and dignified position who hails a cab in the street is at once transformed in my mind into a worthy parent of a family who, after his usual office duties, immediately leaves town and, unencumbered by luggage, hastens to the bosom of his family—to the country; for every passer-by now wears quite a different look, a look which almost seems to say to every person he meets, "As a matter of fact, sir, I'm here by sheer chance, just passing through, you understand, and in a few hours I shall be on the way to the country." If a window is thrown open and a most ravishing young girl, who at a moment ago had been drumming on it with her lovely white fingers, pokes out her pretty head and calls to the man selling pots of plants in the street, I immediately jump to the conclusion that the flowers are bought not for the purpose of enjoying the spring and the flowers in a stuffy old flat in town, for very soon everybody will anyway be leaving for the country and will take even the flowers with them. Why, I've got so far in my new discovery (quite a unique discovery, you must admit) that I can tell at once, just by looking at a man, in what sort of a cottage he lives in the country. The residents of the Stone and Apothecary Islands can be recognised by their studied exquisiteness of manners, their smart summer clothes, and their wonderful carriages in which they come to town. The inhabitants of Pargolov and places beyond "inspire" your confidence at the first glance by their solidly prosperous position and their general air of sobriety and common sense; while the householder of Krestovsky Island is distinguished by his imperturbably cheerful look. Whether I happen to come across a long procession of carters, each walking leisurely, reins in hand, beside his cart, laden with whole mountains of furniture of every description—tables, chairs, Turkish and non-Turkish divans, and other household chattels—and, moreover, often presided over by a frail-looking cook who, perched on the very top of the cart, guards the property of her master as though it were the apple of her eye; or whether I look at the barges, heavily laden with all sorts of domestic junk, sailing on the Neva or the Fontanka, as far as the Black River or the Islands—both carts and barges multiply tenfold, nay, a hundredfold in my eyes. It really seems as though everything had arisen and set off on a journey as though everything were moving off in caravan after caravan into the country; it seems as though the whole of Petersburg were about to turn into a desert, and it is hardly surprising that in the end I am overwhelmed with shame, humiliation, and sadness. For I have no possible excuse for going to the country; neither have I any country cottage I can go to. I am willing to leave with every cart or every gentleman of respectable appearance who hails a cab; but no one, absolutely no one, invites me to go with him, as though they had all forgotten me, as though I were no more than a stranger to them!

I walked for hours and hours, and, as usual, had for some time been completely oblivious of my surroundings, when I suddenly found myself near the toll-gate. I felt cheerful at once, and, stepping beyond the bar, walked along the road between fields of corn and meadows of lush grass, unconscious of any fatigue, and feeling with every breath I drew that a heavy weight was being lifted from my heart. All the travellers I met looked so genially at me that it seemed that in another moment they would most assuredly bow to me. All of them seemed to be happy about something, and every one of them without exception smoked a cigar. And I, too, was happy as never before in my life. As though I had suddenly found myself in Italy—so strong was the impact of nature upon me, a semi-invalid townsman who had all but been stifled within the walls of the city.

There is something indescribably moving in the way nature in Petersburg, suddenly with the coming of spring, reveals herself in all her might and glory, in all the splendour with which heaven has endowed her, in the way she blossoms out, dresses up, decks herself out with flowers. . . . She reminds me somehow rather forcibly of that girl, ailing and faded, upon whom you sometimes look with pity or with a certain compassionate affection, or whom you simply do not notice at all, but who in the twinkling of an eye and only for one fleeting moment becomes by some magic freak of chance indescribably fair and beautiful; and, stunned and fascinated, you ask yourself what power it was that made those sad and wistful eyes blaze forth with such a fire? What caused the rush of blood to her pale and hollow cheeks? What brought passion to that sweet face? Why did her bosom heave so wildly? What was it that so instantaneously suffused the face of the poor girl with life, vigour, and beauty? What forced it to light up with so brilliant a smile? What animated it with so warm, so infectious a laugh? You look round; you wonder who it could have been; you begin to suspect the truth. But the brief moment passes, and tomorrow perhaps you will again encounter the same wistful and forlorn gaze, the same wan face, the same resignation and diffidence in her movements, and, yes, even remorse, even traces of some benumbing vexation and despondency for that brief outburst of passion. And you feel sorry that the beauty, so momentarily evoked, should have faded so quickly and so irrevocably, that she should have burst upon your sight so deceptively and to so little purpose—that she should not have given you time even to fall in love with her. . . .

But all the same my night was much better than the day! This is how it happened:

I came back to town very late, and, as I was approaching the street where I lived, it struck ten. My way lay along a canal embankment where not a single living soul could be seen at that hour. It is true, I live in a very remote part of the town. I was walking along and singing, for when I am happy I always hum some tune to myself like every happy man who has neither friends nor good acquaintances, and who has no one to share his joy with in a moment of happiness. Suddenly I became involved in a most unexpected adventure.

A little distance away, leaning against the railing of the canal, a woman was standing with her elbows on the rail; she seemed to be engrossed in looking at the muddy water of the canal. She wore a most enchanting yellow hat and a very charming black cloak. "She's young," I thought, "and I'm sure she is dark." She did not seem to hear my footsteps, for she did not stir when I walked past her with bated breath and a thumping heart. "Funny!" I thought, "she must be thinking about something very important." Suddenly I stopped dead, rooted to the spot. The sound of suppressed weeping reached me. No, I was not mistaken. The girl was crying, for a minute later I distinctly heard her sobbing again. Good gracious! My heart contracted with pity. And timid though I am with women, this was too good a chance to be missed! . . . I retraced my steps, walked up to her, and in another moment would have certainly said "Madam!" if I had not known that that exclamation had been made a thousand times before in all Russian novels of high life. It was that alone that stopped me. But while I was searching for the right word with which to address the girl, she had recovered her composure, recollected herself, lowered her eyes, and darted past me along the embankment. I immediately set off in pursuit of her, but she must have guessed my intention, for she left the embankment and, crossing the road, walked along the pavement. I did not dare to cross the road. My heart was fluttering like the heart of a captured bird. But quite an unexpected incident came to my assistance.

A gentleman in evening dress suddenly appeared a few yards away from the girl on the other side of the street. He had reached the age of discretion, but there was no discretion in his unsteady gait. He was walking along, swaying from side to side, and leaning cautiously against a wall. The girl, on the other hand, walked as straight as an arrow, quickly and apprehensively, as girls usually walk at night when they do not want any man to offer to accompany them home. And the reeling gentleman would most certainly not have caught up with her, if my good luck had not prompted him to resort to a stratagem. Without uttering a word, he suddenly set off in pursuit of the girl at an amazing speed. She was running away from him as fast as her legs would carry her, but the staggering gentleman was getting nearer and nearer, and then caught up with her. The girl uttered a shriek and—I have to thank my good genius for the excellent knobbly walking-stick which, as it happened, I was at the time clutching in my right hand. In less than no time I found myself on the other side of the street, and in less than no time the unwelcome gentleman took in the situation, took into account the undeniable fact of my superior weapons, grew quiet, dropped behind, and it was only when we were far away that he bethought himself of protesting against my action in rather forceful terms. But his words hardly reached us.

"Give me your arm," I said to the girl, "and he won't dare to molest you any more."

She silently gave me her arm, which was still trembling with excitement and terror. Oh, unwelcome stranger! How I blessed you at that moment! I stole a glance at her—I was right! She was a most charming girl and dark, too. On her black eyelashes there still glistened the tears of her recent fright or her recent unhappiness—I did not know which. But there was already a gleam of a smile on her lips. She, too, stole a glance at me, blushed a little, and dropped her eyes.

"Well, you see, you shouldn't have driven me away before, should you? If I'd been here, nothing would have happened."

"But I didn't know you. I thought that you too . . ."

"But what makes you think you know me now?"

"Well, I know you a little. Now why, for instance, are you trembling?"

"So you've guessed at once the sort of man I am," I replied, overjoyed that the girl was so intelligent (this is never a fault in a beautiful girl). "Yes, you've guessed at once the sort of man I am. It's quite true, I'm afraid, I'm awfully shy with women, and I don't want to deny that I'm a little excited now, no less than you were a moment ago when that fellow scared you. Yes, I seem to be scared now. It's as though it were all happening to me in a dream, except that even in a dream I did not expect ever to be talking to any woman."

"How do you mean? Not really?"

"Yes, really. You see, if my arm is trembling now, it's because it has never before been clasped by such a pretty little hand as yours. I've entirely lost the habit of talking to women. I mean, I never really was in the habit of talking to them. You see, I'm such a lonely creature. Come to think of it, I don't believe I know how to talk to women. Even now I haven't the faintest idea whether I've said anything to you that I shouldn't. Please tell me frankly if I ever do. I promise you I shan't take offence."

"No, I don't think you've said anything you shouldn't. And if you really want me to be frank with you, I don't mind telling you that women rather like shy men like you. And if you want me to speak more frankly, I like it too, and I promise not to send you away till we reach my home."

"I'm afraid," I began, breathless with excitement, "you'll make me lose my shyness at once, and then goodbye to all my schemes!"

"Devices? What schemes, and what for? I must say that isn't nice at all."

"I beg your pardon. I'm awfully sorry. It was a slip of the tongue. But how can you expect me at this moment not to wish. . . ."

"To make a good impression, you mean?"

"Well, yes. And do, for goodness' sake, be fair. Just think— who am I? At twenty-six—yes, I'm twenty-six— I've never really known anyone. So how can you expect me to speak well, cleverly, and to the point? You, too, I think, would prefer us to be straightforward and honest with each other, wouldn't you? I just can't be silent when my heart is moved to speak. Well, anyway . . . I know you'll hardly believe me, but I've never spoken to any woman, never! Never known one, either! I only dream that some day I shall meet someone at last. Oh, if only you knew how many times I've fallen in love like that!"

"But how? Who with?"

"With no one, of course. Just with my ideal, with the woman I see in my dreams. I make up all sorts of romantic love stories in my dreams. Oh, you don't know the sort of man I am! It's true I have known two or three women—you can't help that, can you?—but what sort of women were they? They were all so mercenary that . . . But let me tell you something really funny, let me tell you how several times I longed to talk to a society lady in the street, I mean, talk to her when she was alone, and without any formality. Very humbly, of course, very respectfully, very passionately. Tell her how horribly depressed I am by my lonely life; ask her not to send me away; explain to her that I have no other way of knowing what a woman is like; suggest to her that it is really her duty as a woman not to reject the humble entreaty of an unhappy man like me; finally, explain to her that all I want of her is that she should say a few friendly words to me, say them with sympathy and understanding, that she should not send me away at once, that she should believe my protestations, that she should listen to what I had to tell her, laugh at me by all means, if she wanted to, but also hold out some hope to me, just say two words to me, and then we need not see each other again! But you're laughing. . . . Well, as a matter of fact, I only said that to make you laugh. . . ."

"Don't be cross with me. I'm laughing because you are your own enemy, and if you had tried you would, I'm sure, have perhaps succeeded, even though it all happened in the street. The simpler, the better. Not one kind-hearted woman, provided, of course, she was not a fool, or angry at something at the time, would have the heart to send you away without saying the two words you were so humbly asking for. But I may be wrong. She would most likely have taken you for a madman. I'm afraid I was judging by myself. I know very well, I assure you, how people live in the world!"

"Thank you," I cried, "thank you a thousand times! you don't know how much I appreciate what you've just done for me!"

"All right, all right! Only tell me how did you guess I'm one of those women with whom . . . well, whom you thought worthy . . . of your attention and friendship. I mean, not a mercenary one, as you call it. What made you decide to come up to me?"

"What made me do that? Why, you were alone, and that fellow was much too insolent. It all happened at night, too, and you must admit it was my duty. . . ."

"No, no! I mean before. On the other side of the street. You wanted to come up to me, didn't you?"

"On the other side of the street? Well, I really don't know what to say. I'm afraid I . . . You see, I was so happy today. I was walking along and singing. I had spent the day in the country. I don't remember ever having experienced such happy moments before. You were . . . However, I may have been mistaken. Please, forgive me, if I remind you of it, but I thought you were crying, and I—I couldn't bear to hear it—I felt miserable about it. But, goodness, had I no right to feel anxious about you? Was it wrong of me to feel a brotherly compassion for you? I'm sorry, I said compassion . . . Well, what I meant was that I couldn't possibly have offended you because I had an impulse to go up to you, could I?"

"Don't say anything more, please," said the girl pressing my hand and lowering her head. "I'm to blame for having started talking about it. But I'm glad I was not mistaken in you. Well, I'm home now. I live in that lane, only two steps from here. Goodbye and thank you."

"But shall we never see each other again? Surely, surely, you can't mean it. Surely, this can't be our last meeting?"

"Well, you see," the girl said, laughing, "at first you only asked for two words, and now. . . . However, I don't think I'd better make any promises. Perhaps we'll meet again."

"I'll be here tomorrow," I said. "Oh, I'm sorry, I seem to be already making demands. . . ."

"Yes, you are rather impatient, aren't you? You're almost making demands. . . ."

"Listen to me, please, listen to me!" I interrupted. "You won't mind if I say something to you again, something of the same kind, will you? It's this: I can't help coming here tomorrow. I am a dreamer. I know so little of real life that I just can't help reliving such moments as these in my dreams, for such moments are something I have very rarely experienced. I am going to dream about you the whole night, the whole week, the whole year. I'll most certainly come here tomorrow. Yes, here, at this place and at this hour. And I shall be happy to remember what happened to me today. Already this place is dear to me. I've two or three places like this in Petersburg. Once I even wept because I remembered something, just as you—I mean, I don't know of course, but perhaps you too were crying ten minutes ago because of some memory. I'm awfully sorry, I seem to have forgotten myself again. Perhaps you were particularly happy here once. . . ."

"Very well," said the girl, "I think I will come here tomorrow, also at ten o'clock. And I can see that I can't possibly forbid you to come, can I? You see, I have to be here. Please don't imagine that I am making an appointment with you. I hope you'll believe me when I say that I have got to be here on some business of my own. Oh, very well, I'll be frank with you: I shan't mind at all if you come here too. To begin with, something unpleasant may happen again as it did today, but never mind that . . . I mean, I'd really like to see you again to—to say two words to you. But, mind, don't think ill of me now, will you? Don't imagine I'm making appointments with men so easily. I wouldn't have made it with you, if. . . . But let that be my secret. Only first you must promise. . . ."

"I promise anything you like!" I cried, delighted. "Only say it. Tell me anything beforehand. I agree to everything. I'll do anything you like. I can answer for myself. I'll be obedient, respectful. . . . You know me, don't you?"

"Well, it's because I know you that I'm asking you to come tomorrow," said the girl, laughing. "I know you awfully well. But, mind, if you come it's on condition that, first (only you will do what I ask you, won't you?—You see, I'm speaking frankly to you), don't fall in love with me. That's impossible, I assure you. I'm quite ready to be your friend. I am, indeed. But you mustn't fall in love with me. So please, don't."

"I swear to you . . ." I cried, seizing her hand.

"No, no. I don't want any solemn promises. I know you're quite capable of flaring up like gunpowder. Don't be angry with me for speaking to you like this. If you knew. . . . You see, I haven't got anyone, either, to whom to say a word, or whom to ask for advice. Of course, it's silly to expect advice from people one meets in the street, but you are different. I feel I know you so well that I couldn't have known you better if we'd been friends for twenty years. You won't fail me, will you?"

"You can depend on me! The only thing is I don't know how I shall be able to survive for the next twenty-four hours."

"Have a good sleep. Good night, and remember I've already confided in you. But, as you expressed it so well a few minutes ago, one hasn't really to account for every feeling, even for brotherly sympathy, has one? You put it so nicely that I felt at once that you're the sort of person I could confide in."

"For goodness' sake, tell me what it is. Please do."

"No, I think you'd better wait till tomorrow. Let it remain a secret for the time being. So much the better for you: at least from a distance it will seem more like a romance. Perhaps I'll tell you tomorrow, perhaps I won't. I'd like to have a good talk to you first, get to know you better...."

"All right, I'll tell you all about myself tomorrow. But, good Lord, the whole thing is just like a miracle! Where am I? Tell me, aren't you glad you weren't angry with me, as some other women might well have been? Only two minutes, and you've made me happy for ever. Yes, happy. Who knows, perhaps you've reconciled me with myself, resolved all my doubts. Perhaps there are moments when I . . . But I'll tell you all about it tomorrow. You shall know everything, everything...."

"All right, I agree. I think you'd better start first."

"Very well."

"Goodbye!"

"Goodbye!"

And we parted. I walked about all night. I couldn't bring myself to go home. I was so happy! Till tomorrow!

Second Night

"Well, so you have survived, haven't you?" she said to me, laughing and pressing both my hands.

"I've been here for the last two hours. You don't know what I've been through today!"

"I know, I know—but to business. Do you know why I've come? Not to talk a lot of nonsense as we did yesterday. You see, we must be more sensible in future. I thought about it a lot yesterday."

"But how? How are we to be more sensible? Not that I have anything against it. But, really, I don't believe anything more sensible has ever happened to me than what's happening to me at this moment."

"Oh? Well, first of all, please don't squeeze my hands like that. Secondly, let me tell you I've given a lot of thought to you today."

"Have you? Well, and what decision have you come to?"

"What decision? Why, that we ought to start all over again. For today I've come to the conclusion that I don't know you at all, that I've behaved like a child, like a silly girl, and of course in the end I blamed my own good heart for everything. I mean, I finished up, as everybody always does when they start examining their own motives, by passing a vote of thanks to myself. And so, to correct my mistake, I've made up my mind to find out all about you to the last detail. But as there's no one I can ask about you, you'll have to tell me everything yourself. Everything, absolutely everything! To begin with, what sort of man are you? Come on, start, please! Tell me the story of your life."

"The story of my life?" I cried, thoroughly alarmed. "But who told you there was such a story? I'm afraid there isn't any."

"But how did you manage to live, if there is no story?" she interrupted me, laughing.

"Without any stories whatsoever! I have lived, as they say, entirely independently. I mean by myself. Do you know what it means to live by oneself?"

"How do you mean by yourself? Do you never see anyone at all?"

"Why, no. I see all sorts of people, but I'm alone all the same."

"Don't you ever talk to anyone?"

"Strictly speaking, never."

"But who are you? Please explain. But wait: I think I can guess. You've probably got a grandmother like me. She's blind, my granny is, and she never lets me go out anywhere, so that I've almost forgotten how to talk to people. And when I behaved badly about two years ago and she saw that there was no holding me, she called me in and pinned my dress to hers—and since then we've sat pinned to one another like that for days and days. She knits a stocking, blind though she is, and I have to sit beside her sewing or reading a book to her. It's a funny sort of situation to be in—pinned to a person for two years or more."

"Good gracious, what bad luck! No, I haven't got such a grandmother."

"If you haven't, why do you sit at home all the time?"

"Look here, do you want to know who I am?"

"Yes, of course!"

"In the strict meaning of the word?"

"Yes, in the strictest meaning of the word!"

"Very well, I'm a character."

"A character? What kind of a character?" the girl cried, laughing merrily, as though she had not laughed for a whole year. "I must say, you're certainly great fun! Look, here's a seat. Let's sit down. No one ever comes this way, so no one will overhear us. Well, start your story, please! For you'll never convince me that you haven't got one. You're just trying to conceal it. Now, first of all, what is a character?"

"A character? Well, it's an original, a queer chap," I said, and, infected by her childish laughter, I burst out laughing myself. "It's a kind of freak. Listen, do you know what a dreamer is?"

"A dreamer? Of course I know. I'm a dreamer myself! Sometimes when I'm sitting by Granny I get all sorts of queer ideas into my head. I mean, once you start dreaming, you let your imagination run away with you, so that in the end I even marry a prince of royal blood! I don't know, it's very nice sometimes— dreaming, I mean. But, on the whole, perhaps it isn't. Especially if you have lots of other things to think of," the girl added, this time rather seriously.

"Fine! Once you're married to an emperor, you will, I think, understand me perfectly. Well, listen——but don't you think I ought to know your name before starting on the story of my life?"

"At last! It took you a long time to think of it, didn't it?"

"Good lord! I never thought of it. You see, I was so happy anyway."

"My name's Nastenka."

"Nastenka! Is that all?"

"Yes, that's all. Isn't it enough for you, you insatiable person?"

"Not enough? Why, not at all. It's more than I expected, much more than I expected, Nastenka, my dear, dear girl, if I may call you by your pet name, if from the very first you—you become Nastenka to me!"

"I'm glad you're satisfied at last! Well?"

"Well, Nastenka, just listen what an absurd story it all is."

I sat down beside her, assumed a pedantically serious pose, and began as though reading from a book:

"There are, if you don't happen to know it already, Nastenka, some very strange places in Petersburg. It is not the same sun which shines upon all the other people of the city that looks in there, but quite a different sun, a new sun, one specially ordered for those places, and the light it sheds on everything is also a different, peculiar sort of light. In those places, dear Nastenka, the people also seem to live quite a different life, unlike that which surges all round us, a life which could only be imagined to exist in some faraway foreign country beyond the seven seas, and not at all in our country and in these much too serious times. Well, it is that life which is a mixture of something purely fantastic, something fervently ideal, and, at the same time (alas, Nastenka!), something frightfully prosaic and ordinary, not to say incredibly vulgar."

"My goodness, what an awful introduction! What shall I be hearing next, I wonder?"

"What you will be hearing next, Nastenka (I don't think I shall ever get tired of calling you Nastenka), is that these places are inhabited by strange people—by dreamers. A dreamer—if you must know its exact definition—is not a man, but a sort of creature of the neuter gender. He settles mostly in some inaccessible place, as though anxious to hide in it even from the light of day; and once he gets inside his room, he'll stick to it like a snail, or, at all events, he is in this respect very like that amusing animal which is an animal and a house both at one and the same time and bears the name of tortoise. Why, do you think, is he so fond of his four walls, invariably painted green, grimy, dismal and reeking unpardonably of tobacco smoke? Why does this funny fellow, when one of his new friends comes to visit him (he usually ends up by losing all his friends one by one), why does this absurd person meet him with such an embarrassed look? Why is he so put out of countenance? Why is he thrown into such confusion, as though he had just committed some terrible crime within his four walls? As though he had been forging paper money? Or writing some atrocious poetry to be sent to a journal with an anonymous letter, in which he will explain that, the poet having recently died, he, his friend, deems it his sacred duty to publish his verses? Can you tell me, Nastenka, why the conversation between the two friends never really gets going? Why doesn't laughter or some witty remark escape the lips of the perplexed caller, who had so inopportunely dropped out of the blue, and who at other times is so fond of laughter and all sorts of quips and cranks? And conversations about the fair sex. And other cheerful subjects. And why does the visitor, who is most probably a recent acquaintance and on his first visit—for in this case there will never be a second, and his visitor will never call again—why, I say, does this visitor feel so embarrassed himself? Why, in spite of his wit (if, that is, he has any), is he so tongue-tied as he looks at the disconcerted face of his host, who is, in turn, utterly at a loss and bewildered after his herculean efforts to smooth things over, and fumbles desperately for a subject to enliven the conversation, to convince his host that he, too, is a man of the world, that he too can talk of the fair sex? The host does everything in fact to please the poor man, who seems to have come to the wrong place and called on him by mistake, by at least showing how anxious he is to entertain him. And why does the visitor, having most conveniently remembered a most urgent business appointment which never existed, all of a sudden grab his hat and take his leave, snatching away his hand from the clammy grasp of his host, who, in a vain attempt to recover what is irretrievably lost, is doing his best to show how sorry he is? Why does his friend burst out laughing the moment he finds himself on the other side of the door? Why does he vow never to call on this queer fellow again, excellent fellow though he undoubtedly is? Why at the same time can't he resist the temptation of indulging in the amusing, if rather far-fetched, fancy of comparing the face of his friend during his visit with the expression of an unhappy kitten, roughly handled, frightened, and subjected to all sorts of indignities, by children who had treacherously captured and humiliated it? A kitten that hides itself away from its tormentors under a chair, in the dark, where, left in peace at last, it cannot help bristling up, spitting, and washing its insulted face with both paws for a whole hour, and long afterwards looking coldly at life and nature and even the bits saved up for it from the master's table by a sympathetic housekeeper?"

"Now, look," interrupted Nastenka, who had listened to me all the time in amazement, opening her eyes and pretty mouth, "look, I haven't the faintest idea why it all happened and why you should ask me such absurd questions. All I know is that all these adventures have most certainly happened to you, and exactly as you told me."

"Indubitably," I replied, keeping a very straight face.

"Well," said Nastenka, "if it's indubitably, then please go on, for I'm dying to hear how it will all end."

"You want to know, Nastenka, what our hero did in his room, or rather what I did in my room, since the hero of this story is none other than my own humble self? You want to know why I was so alarmed and upset for a whole day by the unexpected visit of a friend? You want to know why I was in everyone is hurrying home to dinner, to lie down, to have a rest, and as they walk along they think of other pleasant ways of spending the evening, the night, and the rest of their leisure time. At that hour our hero—for I must ask your permission, Nastenka, to tell my story in the third person, for one feels awfully ashamed to tell it in the first—and so at that hour our hero, who has not been wasting his time, either, is walking along with the others. But a strange expression of pleasure plays on his pale and slightly crumpled-looking face. It is not with indifference that he looks at the sunset which is slowly fading on the cold Petersburg sky. When I say he looks, I'm telling a lie: he does not look at it, but is contemplating it without, as it were, being aware of it himself, as though he were tired or preoccupied at the same time with some other more interesting subject, being able to spare only a passing and almost unintentional glance at what is taking place around him. He is glad to have finished till next day with all tiresome *business*. He is happy as a schoolboy who has been let out of the classroom and is free to devote all his time to his favourite games and forbidden pastimes. Take a good look at him, Nastenka: you will at once perceive that his feeling of joy has had a pleasant effect on his weak nerves and his morbidly excited imagination. Look! he is thinking of something. Of dinner perhaps? Or how he's going to spend the evening? what is he looking at like that? At the gentleman of the solidly prosperous exterior who is bowing so picturesquely to the lady who drives past in a splendid carriage drawn by a pair of mettlesome horses? No, Nastenka, what do all those trivial things matter to him now? He is rich beyond compare with his *own individual* life; he has become rich in the twinkling of an eye, as it were, and it was not for nothing that the farewell ray of the setting sun flashed so gaily across his vision and called forth a whole swarm of impressions from his glowing heart. Now he hardly notices the road on which at any other time every trivial detail would have attracted his attention. Now 'the Goddess of Fancy' (if you have read your Zhukovsky, dear Nastenka) has already spun the golden warp with her wanton hand and is at this very moment weaving patterns of a wondrous, fantastic life before his mind's eye—and, who knows, maybe has transported him with her wanton hand to the seventh crystalline sphere from the excellent granite pavement on which he is now wending his way home. Try stopping him now, ask him suddenly where he is standing now, through what streets he has been walking, and it is certain he will not be able to remember anything, neither where he has been, nor where he is standing now, and, flushing with vexation, he will most certainly tell some lie to save appearances. That is why he starts violently, almost crying out, and looks round in horror when a dear old lady stops him in the middle of the pavement and politely asks him the way. Frowning with vexation, he walks on, scarcely aware of the passers-by who smile as they look at him and turn round to follow him with their eyes. He does not notice the little girl who, after timidly making way for him, bursts out laughing as she gazes at his broad, contemplative smile and wild gesticulations. And still the same fancy in her frolicsome flight catches up the old lady, the passers-by, the laughing little girl, and the bargees who have settled down to their evening meal on the barges which dam up the Fontanka (our hero, let us suppose, is walking along the Fontanka Embankment at that moment), and playfully weaves everybody and everything into her canvas, like a fly in a spider's web. And so, with fresh food for his fancy to feed on, the queer remorse, and unconstrained grief. But so long as that perilous time is not yet—he desires nothing, for he is above all desire, for he is sated, for he is the artist of his own life, which he re-creates in himself to suit whatever new fancy he pleases. And how easily, how naturally, is this imaginary, fantastic world created! As though it were not a dream at all! Indeed, he is sometimes ready to believe that all this life is not a vision conjured up by his overwrought mind, not a mirage, nor a figment of the imagination, but something real, something that actually exists! Why, Nastenka, why, tell me, does one feel so out of breath at such moments? Why—through what magic? through what strange whim?—is the pulse quickened, do tears gush out of the eyes of the dreamer? Why do his pale, moist cheeks burn? Why is all his being filled with such indescribable delight? Why is it that long, sleepless nights pass, as though they were an infinitesimal fraction of time, in unending joy and happiness? And why, when the rising sun casts a rosy gleam through the window and fills the gloomy room with its uncertain, fantastic light, as it so often does in Petersburg, does our dreamer, worn out and exhausted, fling himself on the bed and fall asleep, faint with the raptures of his morbidly overwrought spirit, and with such a weary, languorously sweet ache in his heart? No, Nastenka, you can't help deceiving yourself, you can't help persuading yourself that his soul is stirred by some true, some genuine passion, you can't help believing that there is something alive and palpable in his vain and empty dreams! And what a delusion it all is! Now, for instance, love pierces his heart with all its boundless rapture, with all its pains and agonies. Only look at him and you will be convinced. Can you, looking at him, Nastenka, believe that he really never knew her whom he loved so dearly in his frenzied dream? Can it be that he has only seen her in ravishing visions, and that his passion has been nothing but an illusion? Can it be that they have never really spent so many years of their lives together, hand in hand, alone, just the two of them renouncing the rest of the world, and each of them entirely preoccupied with their own world, their own life? Surely it is she who at the hour of their parting, late at night, lies grieving and sobbing on his bosom, unmindful of the raging storm beneath the relentless sky, unmindful of the wind that snatches and carries away the tears from her dark eyelashes! Surely all this is not a dream— this garden, gloomy, deserted, run wild, with its paths overgrown with weeds, dark and secluded, where they used to walk so often together, where they used to hope, grieve, love, love each other so well, so tenderly and so well! And this queer ancestral mansion, where she has spent so many years in solitude and sadness with her morose old husband, always silent and ill-tempered, who frightened them, who were as timid as children, and who in their fear and anguish hid their love from each other. What misery they suffered, what pangs of terror! How innocent, how pure their love was, and (I need hardly tell you, Nastenka) how malicious people were! And why, of course, he meets her afterwards, far from his native shores, beneath the scorching southern sky of an alien land, in the wonderful Eternal City, amid the dazzling splendours of a ball, to the thunder of music, in a *palazzo* (yes, most certainly in a *palazzo* flooded with light, on the balcony wreathed in myrtle and roses, where, recognising him, she hastily removes her mask, and whispering, 'I'm free!' breaks into sobs and flings herself trembling in his arms. And with a cry of rapture, clinging to each other, they at once forget their unhappiness, their parting, all their sufferings, the dismal house, the old man, the gloomy garden in their far-away country, and the seat on which, with a last passionate kiss, she tore herself away from his arms, numbed with anguish and despair. . . . Oh, you must agree, Nastenka, that anyone would start, feel embarrassed, and blush like a schoolboy who has just stuffed in his pocket an apple stolen from a neighbour's garden, if some stalwart, lanky fellow, a fellow fond of a joke and merry company, opened your door and shouted, 'Hullo, old chap, I've just come from Pavlovsk!' Good Lord! The old count is dying, ineffable bliss is close at hand—and here people come from Pavlovsk!"

Having finished my pathetic speech, I lapsed into no less pathetic a silence. I remember I wished terribly that I could, somehow, in spite of myself, burst out laughing, for I was already feeling that a wicked little devil was stirring within me, that my throat was beginning to tighten, my chin to twitch, and my eyes to fill with tears. I expected Nastenka, who listened to me with wide-open, intelligent eyes, to break into her childish and irresistibly gay laughter. I was already regretting that I had gone too far, that I had been wasting my time in telling her what had been accumulating for so long a time in my heart, and about which I could speak as though I had it all written down—because I had long ago passed judgment on myself, and could not resist the temptation to read it out loud, though I admit I never expected to be understood. But to my surprise she said nothing, and, after a pause, pressed my hand gently and asked with timid sympathy:

"Surely you haven't lived like that all your life, have you?"

"Yes, Nastenka, all my life," I replied, "all my life, and I'm afraid I shall go on like that to the very end."

that I have lost all touch with life, all understanding of what is real and actual; because, finally, I have cursed myself; because already after my fantastic nights I have moments of returning sanity, moments which fill me with horror and dismay! You see, I can't help being aware of the crowd being whirled with a roaring noise in the vortex of life, I can't help hearing and seeing people living real lives. I realise that their life is not made to order, that their life will not vanish like a dream, like a vision; that their life is eternally renewing itself, that it is eternally young, that not one hour of it is like another! No! Timid fancy is dreary and monotonous to the point of drabness. It is the slave of every shadow, of every idea. The slave of the first cloud that of a sudden drifts across the sun and reduces every Petersburg heart, which values the sun so highly, to a state of morbid melancholy—and what is the use of fancy when one is plunged into melancholy! You feel that this *inexhaustible* fancy grows weary at last and exhausts itself from the never-ending strain. For, after all, you do grow up, you do outgrow your ideals, which turn to dust and ashes, which are shattered into fragments; and if you have no other life, you just have to build one up out of these fragments. And meanwhile your soul is all the time craving and longing for something else. And in vain does the dreamer rummage about in his old dreams, raking them over as though they were a heap of cinders, looking in these cinders for some spark, however tiny, to fan it into a flame so as to warm his chilled blood by it and revive in it all that he held so dear before, all that touched his heart, that made his blood course through his veins, that drew tears from his eyes, and that so splendidly deceived him! Do you realise, Nastenka, how far things have gone with me? Do you know that I'm forced now to celebrate the anniversary of my own sensations, the anniversary of that which was once so dear to me, but which never really existed? For I keep this anniversary in memory of those empty, foolish dreams! I keep it because even those foolish dreams are no longer there, because I have nothing left with which to replace them, for even dreams, Nastenka, have to be replaced by something! Do you know that I love to call to mind and revisit at certain dates the places where in my own fashion I was once so happy? I love to build up my present in harmony with my irrevocably lost past; and I often wander about like a shadow, aimlessly and without purpose, sad and dejected, through the alleys and streets of Petersburg. What memories they conjure up! For instance, I remember that exactly a year ago, at exactly this hour, on this very pavement, I wandered about cheerlessly and alone just as I did today. And I can't help remembering that at the time, too, my dreams were sad and dreary, and though I did not feel better then I somehow can't help feeling that it was better, that life was more peaceful, that at least I was not then obsessed by the black thoughts that haunt me now, that I did not suffer from these gloomy and miserable qualms of conscience which now give me no rest either by day or by night. And you ask yourself—where are your dreams? And you shake your head and murmur: how quickly time flies! And you ask yourself again—what have you done with your time, where have you buried the best years of your life? Have you lived or not? Look, you say to yourself, look how everything in the world is growing cold. Some more years will pass, and they will be followed by cheerless solitude, and then will come tottering old age, with its crutch, and after it despair and desolation. Your fantastic world will fade away,

"No, no," Nastenka interrupted, laughing, "it isn't only good advice that I want. I also want warm, brotherly advice, just as though you'd been fond of me for ages!"

"Agreed, Nastenka, agreed!" I cried with enthusiasm. "And if I'd been fond of you for twenty years, I couldn't have been fonder of you than I am now!"

"Your hand!" said Nastenka.

"Here it is!" I replied, giving her my hand.

"Very well, let's begin my story!"

Nastenka's Story

"Half my story you know already, I mean, you know that I have an old grandmother."

"If the other half is as short as this one——" I interrupted, laughing.

"Be quiet and listen. First of all you must promise not to interrupt me, or I shall get confused. Well, please listen quietly.

"I have an old grandmother. I've lived with her ever since I was a little girl, for my mother and father are dead. I suppose my grandmother must have been rich once, for she likes to talk of the good old days. It was she who taught me French and afterwards engaged a teacher for me. When I was fifteen (I'm seventeen now) my lessons stopped. It was at that time that I misbehaved rather badly. I shan't tell you what I did. It's sufficient to say that my offence was not very great. Only Granny called me in one morning and saying that she couldn't look after me properly because she was blind, she took a safety-pin and pinned my dress to hers. She told me that if I didn't mend my ways, we should remain pinned to each other for the rest of our lives. In short, at first, I found it quite impossible to get away from her: my work, my reading, and my lessons had all to be done beside my grandmother. I did try to trick her once by persuading Fyokla to sit in my place. Fyokla is our maid. She is very deaf. Well, so Fyokla took my place. Granny happened to fall asleep in her arm-chair at the time, and I ran off to see a friend of mine who lives close by. But, I'm afraid, it all ended most disastrously. Granny woke up while I was out and asked for something, thinking that I was still sitting quietly in my place. Fyokla saw of course that Granny wanted something, but could not tell what it was. She wondered and wondered what to do and in the end undid the pin and ran out of the room. . . ."

Here Nastenka stopped and began laughing. I, too, burst out laughing with her, which made her stop at once.

"Look, you mustn't laugh at Granny. I'm laughing because it was so funny. . . . Well, anyway, I'm afraid it can't be helped. Granny is like that, but I do love the poor old dear a little for all that. Well, I did catch it properly that time. I was at once told to sit down in my old place, and after that I couldn't make a move without her noticing it.

"Oh, I forgot to tell you that we live in our own house, I mean, of course, in Granny's house. It's a little wooden house, with only three windows, and it's as old as Granny herself. It has an attic, and one day a new lodger came to live in the attic. . . ."

"There was an old lodger then?" I remarked, by the way.

"Yes, of course, there was an old lodger," replied Nastenka, "and let me tell you, he knew how to hold his tongue better than you. As a matter of fact, he hardly ever used it at all. He was a very dried up old man, dumb, blind and lame, so that in the end he just could not go on living and died. Well, of course, we had to get a new lodger, for we can't live without one: the rent we get from our attic together with Granny's pension is almost all the income we have. Our new lodger, as it happened, was a young man, a stranger who had some business in Petersburg. As he did not haggle over the rent, Granny let the attic to him, and then asked me, 'Tell me, Nastenka, what is our lodger like—is he young or old?' I didn't want to tell her a lie, so I said, 'He isn't very young, Granny, but he isn't very old, either.'

" 'Is he good-looking?' Granny asked.

"Again I didn't want to tell her a lie. 'He isn't bad-looking, Granny,' I said. Well, so Granny said, 'Oh dear, that's bad, that's very bad! I tell you this because I don't want you to make a fool of yourself over him. Oh, what terrible times we're living in! A poor lodger and he would be good-looking too! Not like the old days!'

"Granny would have liked everything to be like the old days! She was younger in the old days, the sun was much warmer in the old days, the milk didn't turn so quickly in the old days—everything was so much better in the old days! Well, I just sat there and said nothing, but all the time I was thinking, Why is Granny warning me? Why did she ask whether our lodger was young and good-looking? Well, anyway, the thought only crossed my mind, and soon I was counting my stitches again (I was knitting a stocking at the time), and forgot all about it.

"Well, one morning our lodger came down to remind us that we had promised to paper his room for him. One thing led to another, for Granny likes talking to people and then she told me to go to her bedroom and fetch her accounts. I jumped up, blushed all over—I don't know why—and forgot that I was pinned to Granny. I never thought of undoing the pin quietly, so that our lodger shouldn't notice, but dashed off so quickly that I pulled Granny's armchair after me. When I saw that our lodger knew all about me now, I got red in the face, stopped dead as though rooted to the floor, and suddenly burst into tears. I felt so ashamed and miserable at that moment that I wished I was dead! Granny shouted at me, 'What are you standing there like that for?' But that made me cry worse than ever. When our lodger saw that I was ashamed on account of him, he took his leave and went away at once!

"Ever since that morning I've nearly fainted very time I've heard a noise in the passage. It must be the lodger, I'd think, and I'd undo the pin very quietly just in case it was he. But it never was our lodger. He never came. After a fortnight our lodger sent word with Fyokla that he had a lot of French books, and that they were all good books which he knew we would enjoy reading, and that he would be glad to know whether Granny would like me to choose a book to read to her because he was sure she must be bored. Granny accepted our lodger's kind offer gratefully, but she kept asking me whether the books were *good* books, for if the books were bad, she wouldn't let me read them because she didn't want me to get wrong ideas into my head."

" 'What wrong ideas, Granny? What's wrong with those books?'

" 'Oh,' she said, 'it's all about how young men seduce decent girls, and how on the excuse that they want to marry them, they elope with them and then leave them to their own fate, and how the poor creatures all come to a bad end. I've read a great many such books,' said Granny, 'and everything is described so beautifully in them that I used to keep awake all night, reading them on the quiet. So mind you don't read them, Nastenka,' she said. 'What books has he sent?'

" 'They're all novels by Walter Scott, Granny.'

" 'Walter Scott's novels? Are you certain, Nastenka, there isn't some trickery there? Make sure, dear, he hasn't put a love letter in one of them.'

" 'No, Granny,' I said, 'there's no love letter.'

" 'Oh, dear,' said Granny, 'look in the binding, there's a good girl. Sometimes they stuff it in the binding, the scoundrels.'

" 'No, Granny, there's nothing in the binding.'

" 'Well, that's all right then!'

"So we started reading Walter Scott, and in a month or so we had read through almost half of his novels. Then he sent us some more books. He sent us Pushkin. And in the end I didn't know what to do if I had no book to read and I gave up dreaming of marrying a prince of royal blood.

"So it went on till one day I happened to meet our lodger on the stairs. Granny had sent me to fetch something. He stopped. I blushed and he blushed. However, he laughed, said good morning to me, asked me how Granny was, and then said, 'Well, have you read the books?' I said, 'Yes, we have.' 'Which did you like best?' I said, 'I liked *Ivanhoe* and Pushkin best of all.' That was all that happened that time.

"A week later I again happened to meet him on the stairs. That time Granny had not sent me for anything, but I had gone up to fetch something myself. It was past two in the afternoon, when our lodger usually came home. 'Good afternoon,' he said. 'Good afternoon,' I said.

" 'Don't you feel awfully bored sitting with your Granny all day?' he said.

"The moment he asked me that, I blushed—I don't know why. I felt awfully ashamed, and hurt, too, because I suppose it was clear that even strangers were beginning to wonder how I could sit all day long pinned to my Granny. I wanted to go away without answering, but I just couldn't summon enough strength to do that.

" 'Look here,' he said, 'you're a nice girl, and I hope you don't mind my telling you that I'm more anxious even than your Granny that you should be happy. Have you no girl friends at all whom you'd like to visit?'

"I told him I hadn't any. I had only one, Mashenka, but she had gone away to Pskov.

" 'Would you like to go to the theatre with me?' he asked.

" 'To the theatre? But what about Granny?'

" 'Couldn't you come without her knowing anything about it?'

" 'No, sir,' I said. 'I don't want to deceive my Granny. Goodbye.'

" 'Goodbye,' he said, and went upstairs without another word.

"After dinner, however, he came down to see us. He sat down and had a long talk with Granny. He asked her whether she ever went out, whether she had any friends, and then suddenly he said, 'I've taken a box for the opera for this evening. They're giving *The Barber of Seville*. Some friends of mine wanted to come, but they couldn't manage it, and now the tickets are left on my hands.'

" '*The Barber of Seville*!' cried my Granny. 'Why, is it the same barber they used to act in the old days?'

" 'Yes,' he replied, 'it's the same barber,' and he glanced at me.

"Of course I understood everything. I blushed and my heart began thumping in anticipation.

" 'Oh,' said Granny, 'I know all about him! I used to play Rosina myself in the old days at private theatricals.'

" 'Would you like to go today?' said the lodger. 'My ticket will be wasted if nobody comes.'

" 'Yes, I suppose we could go,' said Granny. 'Why shouldn't we? My Nastenka has never been to a theatre before.'

"My goodness, wasn't I glad! We started getting ready at once, put on our best clothes, and went off. Granny couldn't see anything, of course, because she is blind, but she wanted to hear the music, and, besides, she's really very kind-hearted, the old dear. She wanted me to go and enjoy myself, for we would never have gone by ourselves. Well, I won't tell you what my impression of *The Barber of Seville* was. I'll merely mention that our lodger looked at me so nicely the whole evening, and he spoke so nicely to me that I guessed at once that he had only meant to try me out in the afternoon, to see whether I would have gone with him alone. Oh, I was so happy! I went to bed feeling so proud, so gay, and my heart was beating so fast that I felt a little feverish and raved all night about *The Barber of Seville*.

"I thought he'd come and see us more and more often after that, but it turned out quite differently. He almost stopped coming altogether. He'd come down once a month, perhaps, and even then only to invite us to the theatre. We went twice to the theatre with him. Only I wasn't a bit happy about it. I could see that he was simply sorry for me because I was treated so abominably by my grandmother and that otherwise he wasn't interested in me at all. So it went on till I couldn't bear it any longer: I couldn't sit still for a minute, I couldn't read anything, I couldn't work. Sometimes I'd burst out laughing and do something just to annoy Granny, and sometimes I'd just burst into tears. In the end I got terribly thin and was nearly ill. The opera season was over, and our lodger stopped coming down to see us altogether, and when we did meet—always on the stairs, of course—he'd just bow to me silently, and look very serious as though he did not want to talk to me, and he'd be out on the front steps while I'd still be standing halfway up the stairs, red as a cherry, for every time I met him all my blood rushed to my head.

"Well, I've almost finished. Just a year ago, in May, our lodger came down to our drawing-room and told Granny that he had finished his business in Petersburg and was leaving for Moscow where he would have to stay a whole year. When I heard that I went pale and sank back in my chair as though in a faint. Granny did not notice anything, and he, having told us that he was giving up his room, took his leave and went away.

"What was I to do? I thought and thought, worried and worried, and at last I made up my mind. As he was leaving tomorrow, I decided to make an end to it all after Granny had gone to bed. I tied up all my clothes in a bundle and, more dead than alive, went upstairs with my bundle to see our lodger. I suppose it must have taken me a whole hour to walk up the stairs to the attic. When I opened the door of his room, he cried out as he looked at me. He thought I was a ghost. He quickly fetched a glass of water for me, for I could hardly stand on my feet. My heart was beating very fast, my head ached terribly, and I felt all in a daze. When I recovered a little, I just put my bundle on his bed, sat down beside it, buried my face in my hands, and burst into a flood of tears. He seemed to have understood everything at once, and he stood before me looking so pale and gazing at me so sadly that my heart nearly broke.

" 'Listen, Nastenka,' he said, 'I can't do anything now. I'm a poor man. I haven't got anything at present, not even a decent job. How would we live, if I were to marry you?'

"We talked for a long time, and in the end I worked myself up into a real frenzy and told him that I couldn't go on living with my grandmother any more, that I'd run away from her, that I didn't want to be fastened by a pin all my life, and that, if he liked, I'd go to Moscow with him because I couldn't live without him. Shame, love, pride seemed to speak in me all at once, and I fell on the bed almost in convulsions. I was so afraid that he might refuse to take me!

"He sat in silence for a few minutes, then he got up, went to me, and took me by the hand.

" 'Listen to me, darling Nastenka,' he began, also speaking through his tears, 'I promise you solemnly that if at any time I am in a position to marry, you are the only girl in the world I would marry. I assure you that now you are the only one who could make me happy. Now, listen. I'm leaving for Moscow and I shall be away exactly one year. I hope to settle my affairs by that time. When I come back, and if you still love me, I swear to you that we shall be married. I can't possibly marry you now. It is out of the question. And I have no right to make any promises to you. But I repeat that if I can't marry you after one year, I shall certainly marry you sometime. Provided of course you still want to marry me and don't prefer someone else, for I cannot and I dare not bind you by any sort of promise.'

"That was what he told me, and the next day he left. We agreed not to say anything about it to Granny. He insisted on that. Well, that's almost the end of my story. A year has now passed, exactly one year. He is in Petersburg now, he's been here three days, and—and———"

"And what?" I cried, impatient to hear the end.

"And he hasn't turned up so far," said Nastenka, making a great effort to keep calm. "I haven't heard a word from him."

Here she stopped, paused a little, lowered her pretty head, and, burying her face in her hands, suddenly burst out sobbing so bitterly that my heart bled to hear it.

I had never expected such an ending.

"Nastenka," I began timidly, in an imploring voice, "for goodness sake, Nastenka, don't cry! How can you tell? Perhaps he hasn't arrived yet. . . ."

"He has, he has!" Nastenka exclaimed. "I know he's here. We made an arrangement the night before he left. After our talk we went for a walk here on the embankment. It was ten o'clock. We sat on this seat. I was no longer crying then. I felt so happy listening to him! He said that immediately on his return he would come to see us, and if I still wanted to marry him, we'd tell Granny everything. Well, he's back now, I know he is, but he hasn't come, he hasn't come!"

And once more she burst into tears.

"Good heavens, isn't there anything we can do?" I cried, jumping up from the seat in utter despair. "Tell me, Nastenka, couldn't I go and see him?"

"You think you could?" she said, raising her head.

"No, of course not," I replied, checking myself. "But, look here, why not write him a letter?"

"No, no, that's impossible!" she replied firmly, but lowering her head and not looking at me.

"Why is it impossible? What's wrong with it?" I went on pleading with her, the idea having rather appealed to me. "It all depends what sort of a letter it is, Nastenka. There are letters and letters, and—oh, Nastenka, believe me it's true. Trust me, Nastenka, please! I wouldn't give you bad advice. It can all be arranged. It was you who took the first step, wasn't it? Well, why not now——?"

"No; it's quite impossible! It would look as if I was thrusting myself on him. . . ."

"But, darling Nastenka," I interrupted her, and I couldn't help smiling, "believe me, you're wrong, quite wrong. You're absolutely justified in writing to him, for he made a promise to you. Besides, I can see from what you've told me that he is a nice man, that he has behaved decently," I went on, carried away by the logic of my own reasoning and my own convictions. "For what did he do? He bound himself by a promise. He said that he wouldn't marry anyone but you, if, that is, he ever married at all. But he left you free to decide whether or not you want to marry him, to refuse him at any moment. This being so, there's no reason on earth why you shouldn't make the first move. You're entitled to do so, and you have an advantage over him, if, for instance, you should choose to release him from his promise. . . ."

"Look, how would you have written——?"

"What?"

"Such a letter."

"Well, I'd have started, 'Dear Sir. . . .' "

"Must it begin with 'Dear Sir?' "

"Of course! I mean, not necessarily. . . . You could. . . ."

"Never mind. How would you go on?"

"'Dear Sir, you will pardon me for . . .' No, I don't think you should apologise for writing to him. The circumstances themselves fully justify your letter. Write simply: 'I am writing to you. Forgive me for my impatience, but all the year I have lived in such happy anticipation of your return that it is hardly surprising that I cannot bear the suspense even one day longer. Now that you are back, I cannot help wondering whether you have not after all changed your mind. If that is so, then my letter will tell you that I quite understand and that I am not blaming you for anything. I do not blame you that I have no power over your heart: such seems to be my fate. You are an honourable man. I know you will not be angry with me or smile at my impatience. Remember that it is a poor girl who is writing to you, that she is all alone in the world, that she has no one to tell her what to do or give her any advice, and that she herself never did know how to control her heart. But forgive me that doubt should have stolen even for one moment into my heart. I know that even in your thoughts you are quite incapable of hurting her who loved you so much and who still loves you.'"

"Yes, yes, that's exactly what I was thinking!" Nastenka cried, her eyes beaming with joy. "Oh, you've put an end to all my doubts. I'm sure God must have sent you to me. Thank you, thank you!"

"What are you thanking me for? Because God has sent me to you?" I replied, gazing delighted at her sweet, happy face.

"Yes, for that too."

"Oh, Nastenka, aren't we sometimes grateful to people only because they live with us? Well, I'm grateful to you for having met you. I'm grateful to you because I shall remember you all my life!"

"All right, all right! Now listen to me carefully: I arranged with him that he'd let me know as soon as he came back by leaving a letter for me at the house of some people I know—they are very nice, simple people who know nothing about the whole thing; and that if he couldn't write me a letter because one can't say all one wants in a letter, he'd come here, where we had arranged to meet, at exactly ten o'clock on the very first day of his arrival. Now, I know he has arrived, but for two days he hasn't turned up, nor have I had a letter from him. I can't possibly get away from Granny in the morning. So please take my letter tomorrow to the kind people I told you of, and they'll see that it reaches him. And if there is a reply, you could bring it yourself tomorrow evening at ten o'clock."

"But the letter! What about the letter? You must write the letter first, which means that I couldn't take it before the day after tomorrow."

"The letter . . . ?" said Nastenka, looking a little confused. "Oh, the letter! . . . Well——"

But she didn't finish. At first she turned her pretty face away from me, then she blushed like a rose, and then all of a sudden I felt that the letter which she must have written long before was in my hand. It was in a sealed envelope. A strangely familiar, sweet, lovely memory flashed through my mind.

"Ro-o-si-i-na-a!" I began.

"Rosina!" both of us burst out singing. I almost embraced her with delight, and she blushed as only she could blush and laughed through the tears which trembled on her dark eyelashes like pearls.

"Well, that's enough," she said, speaking rapidly. "Goodbye now. Here's the letter and here's the address where you have to take it. Goodbye! Till tomorrow!"

She pressed both my hands warmly, nodded her head, and darted away down her side-street. I remained standing in the same place for a long time, following her with my eyes.

"Till tomorrow! Till tomorrow!" flashed through my mind as she disappeared from sight.

Third Night

It was a sad and dismal day today, rainy, without a ray of hope, just like the long days of my old age which I know will be as sad and dismal. Strange thoughts are crowding into my head, my heart is full of gloomy forebodings, questions too vague to be grasped clearly fill my mind, and somehow I've neither the power nor the will to resolve them. No, I shall never be able to solve it all!

We are not going to meet today. Last night, when we said goodbye, the sky was beginning to be overcast, and a mist was rising. I observed that the weather did not look too promising for tomorrow, but she made no answer. She did not wish to say anything to cloud her own happy expectations. For her this day is bright and full of sunshine, and not one cloud will obscure her happiness.

"If it rains," she said, "we shan't meet! I shan't come!"

I thought she would not pay any attention to the rain today, but she never came.

Yesterday we had met for the third time. It was our third white night. . . .

But how beautiful people are when they are gay and happy! How brimful of love their hearts are! It is as though they wanted to pour their hearts into the heart of another human being, as though they wanted the whole world to be gay and laugh with them. And how infectious that gaiety is! There was so much joy in her words yesterday, so much goodness in her heart towards me. How sweet she was to me, how hard she tried to be nice to me, how she comforted and soothed my heart! Oh, how sweet a woman can be to you when she is happy! And I? Why, I was completely taken in. I thought she—

But how on earth could I have thought it? How could I have been so blind, when everything had already been taken by another, when nothing belonged to me? Why, even that tenderness of hers, that anxiety, that love—yes, that love for me was nothing more than the outward manifestation of her happiness at the thought of her meeting with someone else, her desire to force her happiness upon me too. When he did not turn up, when we waited in vain, she frowned, she lost heart, she was filled with alarm. All her movements, all her words, seemed to have lost their liveliness, their playfulness, their gaiety. And the strange thing was that she seemed doubly anxious to please me, as though out of an instinctive desire to lavish upon me what she so dearly desired for herself, but what she feared would never be hers. My Nastenka was so nervous and in such an agonising dread that at last she seemed to have realised that I loved her and took pity upon my unhappy love. It is always so: when we are unhappy we feel more strongly the unhappiness of others; our feeling is not shattered, but becomes concentrated. . . .

I came to her with a full heart; I could scarcely wait for our meeting. I had no presentiment of how I would be feeling now.

I little dreamt that it would all end quite differently. She was beaming with happiness. She was expecting an answer to her letter. The answer was he himself. He was bound to come; he had to come running in answer to her call. She arrived a whole hour before me. At first she kept on laughing at everything; every word of mine provoked a peal of laughter from her. I began talking, but lapsed into silence.

"Do you know why I'm so happy?" she said. "Do you know why I'm so glad when I look at you? Do you know why I love you so today?"

"Well?" I asked, and my heart trembled.

"I love you so, because you haven't fallen in love with me. Another man in your place would, I'm sure, have begun to pester me, to worry me. He would have been sighing, he would have looked so pathetic, but you're so sweet!"

Here she clasped my hand with such force that I almost cried out. She laughed.

"Oh, what a good friend you are!" she began a minute later, speaking very seriously. "You're a real godsend to me. What would I have done if you'd not been with me now? How unselfish you are! How truly you love me! When I am married, we shall be such good friends. You'll be more than a brother to me. I shall love you almost as I love him! . . ."

Somehow I couldn't help feeling terribly sad at that moment. However, something resembling laughter stirred in my soul.

"Your nerves are on edge," I said. "You're afraid. You don't think he'll come."

"Goodness, what nonsense you talk!" she said. "If I hadn't been so happy, I do believe I'd have burst out crying to hear you express such doubts, to hear you reproaching me like that. You've given me an idea, though. And I admit you've given me a lot to think about, but I shall think about it later. I don't mind telling you frankly that you're quite right. Yes, I'm not quite myself tonight. I'm in awful suspense, and every little thing jars on me, excites me, but please don't let us discuss my feelings! . . ."

At that moment we heard footsteps, and a man loomed out of the darkness. He was coming in our direction. She almost cried out. I released her hand and made a movement as though I were beginning to back away. But we were both wrong: it was not he.

"What are you so afraid of? Why did you let go of my hand?" she said, giving me her hand again. "What does it matter? We'll meet him together. I want him to see how we love one another."

"How we love one another?" I cried.

"Oh, Nastenka, Nastenka," I thought, "how much you've said in that word! Such love, Nastenka, at certain moments makes one's heart ache and plunges one's spirit into gloom. Your hand is cold, but mine burns like fire. How blind you are, Nastenka! How unbearable a happy person sometimes is! But I'm afraid I could not be angry with you, Nastenka!"

At last my heart overflowed.

"Do you know, Nastenka," I cried, "do you know what I've gone through all day?"

"Why? What is it? Tell me quickly! Why haven't you said anything about it before?"

"Well, first of all, Nastenka, after I had carried out all your commissions, taken the letter, seen your good friends, I—I went home and—and went to bed."

"Is that all?" she interrupted, laughing.

"Yes, almost all," I replied, making an effort to keep calm, for I already felt foolish tears starting to my eyes. "I woke an hour before we were due to meet. But I don't seem to have really slept at all. I don't know how to describe the curious sensation I had. I seemed to be on my way here. I was going to tell you everything. I had an odd feeling as though time had suddenly stopped, as though one feeling, one sensation, would from that moment go on and on for all eternity, as though my whole life had come to a standstill. . . . When I woke up it seemed to me that some snatch of a tune I had known for a long time, I had heard somewhere before but had forgotten, a melody of great sweetness, was coming back to me now. It seemed to me that it had been trying to emerge from my soul all my life, and only now———"

"Goodness," Nastenka interrupted, "what's all this about? I don't understand a word of it."

"Oh, Nastenka, I wanted somehow to convey that strange sensation to you," I began in a plaintive voice, in which there still lurked some hope, though I'm afraid a very faint one.

"Don't, please don't!" she said, and in a trice she guessed everything, the little rogue.

She became on a sudden somehow extraordinarily talkative, gay, playful. She took my arm, laughed, insisted that I should laugh too, and every halting word I uttered evoked a long loud peal of laughter from her. I was beginning to feel angry; she suddenly began flirting.

"Listen," she said, "I'm really beginning to be a little annoyed with you for not being in love with me. What am I to think of you after that? But, sir, if you insist on being so strong-minded, you should at least show your appreciation of me for being such a simple girl. I tell you everything, absolutely everything. Any silly old thing that comes into my head."

"Listen, I think it's striking eleven!" I said, as the clock from some distant city tower began slowly to strike the hour.

She stopped suddenly, left off laughing, and began to count.

"Yes," she said at last in a hesitating, unsteady voice, "its eleven."

I regretted at once that I had frightened her. It was brutal of me to make her count the strokes. I cursed myself for my uncontrolled fit of malice. I felt sorry for her, and I did not know how to atone for my inexcusable behaviour. I did my best to comfort her. I tried hard to think of some excuse for his failure to come. I argued. I reasoned with her. It was the easiest thing in the world to deceive her at that moment! Indeed, who would not be glad of any word of comfort at such a moment? Who would not be overjoyed at the faintest glimmer of an excuse?

"The whole thing's absurd!" I began, feeling more and more carried away by my own enthusiasm and full of admiration for the extraordinary clarity of my own arguments. "He couldn't possibly have come today. You've got me so muddled and confused, Nastenka, that I've lost count of the time. Why, don't you see? He's scarcely had time to receive your letter. Now, suppose that for some reason he can't come today. Suppose he's going to write to you. Well, in that case you couldn't possibly get his letter till tomorrow. I'll go and fetch it for you early tomorrow morning and let you know at once. Don't you see? A thousand things may have happened: he may have been out when your letter arrived, and for all we know he may not have read it even yet. Anything may have happened."

"Yes, yes!" said Nastenka. "I never thought of that. Of course anything may have happened," she went on in a most acquiescent voice, but in which, like some jarring note, another faintly perceptible thought was hidden away. "Yes, please do that. Go there as soon as possible tomorrow morning, and if you get anything let me know at once. You know where I live, don't you?"

And she began repeating her address to me.

Then she became suddenly so sweet, so shy with me. She seemed to listen attentively to what I was saying to her; but when I asked her some question, she made no reply, grew confused, and turned her head away. I peered into her eyes. Why, of course! She was crying.

"How can you? How can you? Oh, what a child you are! What childishness! There, there, stop crying please!"

She tried to smile, to compose herself, but her chin was still trembling, and her bosom still rising and falling.

"I'm thinking of you," she said to me after a minute's silence. "You're so good that I'd have to have a heart of stone not to feel it. Do you know what has just occurred to me? I was comparing the two of you in my mind. Why isn't he you? Why isn't he like you? He's not as good as you, though I love him more than you."

I said nothing in reply. She seemed to be waiting for me to say something.

"Of course it's probably quite true that I don't know him very well. No, I don't understand him very well. You see, I seemed always a little afraid of him. He was always so serious, and I couldn't help thinking proud as well. I realise of course that he merely looked like that. I know there's more tenderness in his heart than in mine. I can't forget the way he looked at me when—you remember?—I came to him with my bundle. But all the same I seem to look up to him a little too much, and that doesn't seem as if we were quite equals, does it?"

"No, Nastenka, no," I replied. "It does not mean that you are not equals. It merely means that you love him more than anything in the world, far more than yourself even."

"Yes, I suppose that is so," said Nastenka. "But do you know what I think? Only I'm not speaking of him now, but just in general. I've been thinking for a long time, why aren't we all just like brothers to one another. Why does even the best of us seem to hide something from other people and keep something back from them? Why don't we say straight out what's in our hearts, if we know that our words will not be spoken in vain? As it is, everyone seems to look as though he were much harder than he really is. It is as though we were all afraid our feelings would be hurt if we revealed them too soon."

"Oh, Nastenka, you're quite right, but there are many reasons for that," I interrupted, for I knew that I myself was suppressing my feelings at that moment more than ever before.

"No, no!" she replied with great feeling. "You, for instance, are not like that. I really don't know how to tell you what I feel. But it seems to me, for instance—I mean I can't help feeling that you—that just at this moment you're making some sacrifice for me," she added shyly, with a quick glance at me. "Please forgive me for telling you that. You know I am such a simple girl. I haven't had much experience of the world and I really don't know sometimes how to express myself," she added in a voice that trembled from some hidden emotion, trying to smile at the same time. "But I just wanted to tell you that I'm grateful, that I'm aware of it too. . . . Oh, may God grant you happiness for that! I feel that what you told me about your dreamer is not true, I mean it has nothing to do with you. You are recovering, you're quite different from the man you described yourself to be. If you ever fall in love, may you be happy with her. I don't need to wish her anything, for she'll be happy with you. I know because I'm a woman myself, so you must believe me when I tell you so."

She fell silent and pressed my hand warmly. I was too moved to say anything. A few minutes passed.

"Yes, it seems he won't come tonight," she said at last, raising her head. "It's late."

"He'll come tomorrow," I said in a very firm, confident voice.

"Yes," she added, looking cheerful again, "I realise myself now that he couldn't possibly come till tomorrow. Well, goodbye! Till tomorrow! I may not come, if it rains. But the day after tomorrow I shall come whatever happens. You'll be here for certain, won't you? I want to see you. I'll tell you everything."

And later, when we said goodbye to each other, she gave me her hand and said, looking serenely at me—

"Now we shall always be together, shan't we?"

Oh, Nastenka, Nastenka, if only you knew how terribly lonely I am now!

When the clock struck nine, I could remain in my room no longer. I dressed and went out in spite of the bad weather. I was there. I sat on our seat. I went to her street, but I felt ashamed and went back when I was only a few yards from her house without even looking at her windows. What a day! Damp and dreary. If it had been fine, I should have walked about all night.

But—till tomorrow, till tomorrow! Tomorrow she'll tell me everything.

There was no letter for her today, though. However, there's nothing surprising in that. They must be together by now. . . .

Fourth Night

Good Lord, how strangely the whole thing has ended! What a frightful ending!

I arrived at nine o'clock. She was already there. I noticed her a long way off. She was standing, leaning with her elbows on the railing of the embankment, just as she had been standing the first time I saw her, and she did not hear me when I came up to her.

"Nastenka!" I called her, restraining my agitation with difficulty.

She turned round to me quickly.

"Well?" she said. "Well? Tell me quickly!"

I looked at her utterly bewildered.

"Well, where's the letter? Haven't you brought the letter?" she repeated, gripping the railing with her hand.

"No, I haven't got any letter," I said at last. "Hasn't he come?"

She turned terribly pale and stared at me for a long time without moving. I had shattered her last hope.

"Well, it doesn't matter," she said at last in a strangled voice. "If he leaves me like that, then perhaps it's best to forget him!"

She dropped her eyes, then tried to look at me, but couldn't do it. For a few more minutes she tried to pull herself together, then she turned away from me suddenly, leaned on the railing with her elbows, and burst into tears.

"Come, come," I began, but as I looked at her I hadn't the heart to go on. And, besides, what could I have said to her?

"Don't try to comfort me," she said, weeping. "Don't tell me he'll come—that he hasn't deserted me so cruelly and so inhumanly as he has. Why? Why did he do it? Surely there was nothing in my letter, in that unhappy letter of mine, was there?"

Here her voice was broken by sobs. My heart bled as I looked at her.

"Oh, how horribly cruel it is!" she began again. "And not a line, not a line! If he'd just written to say that he didn't want me, that he rejected me, but not to write a single line in three days! How easy it is for him to slight and insult a poor defenceless girl whose only fault is that she loves him! Oh, what I've been through these three days! Lord, when I think that it was I who went to him the first time, when I think how I humiliated myself before him, how I cried, how I implored him for a little love! And after that! . . . But, look here," she said, turning to me, and her black eyes flashed, "there's something wrong! There must be something wrong! It's not natural! Either you are mistaken or I am. Perhaps he didn't get my letter. Perhaps he still doesn't know anything. Tell me, for heaven's sake, explain it to me—I can't understand it—how could he have behaved so atrociously to me. Not one word! Why, people show more pity to the lowest creature on earth! Perhaps he has heard something, perhaps someone has told him something about me," she cried, turning to me for an answer: "What do you think?"

"Listen, Nastenka, I'll go and see him tomorrow on your behalf."

"Well?"

"I'll try and find out from him what the position is. I'll tell him everything."

"Well? Well?"

"You write a letter. Don't refuse, Nastenka, don't refuse! I'll make him respect your action. He'll learn everything, and if—"

"No, my friend, no," she interrupted. "Enough! Not another word, not another word from me, not a line—I've had enough! I don't know him any more, I don't love him any more, I'll f-f-forget him."

She did not finish.

"Calm yourself, calm yourself, my dear! Sit here, Nastenka," I said, making her sit down on the seat.

"But I am calm. I tell you this is nothing. It's only tears—they'll soon dry. You don't really think I'm going to do away with myself, drown myself, do you?"

My heart was full: I tried to speak, but I couldn't

"Listen," she said, taking my hand, "you wouldn't have behaved like this, would you? You wouldn't have abandoned a girl who had come to you of her own free will, you wouldn't have made a cruel mockery of her weak foolish heart, would you? You would have taken care of her. You would have reminded yourself that she had nobody in the whole world, that she was so inexperienced, that she could not prevent herself from falling in love with you, that she couldn't help it, that it wasn't her fault—no, it wasn't her fault!—that she had not done anything wrong. Oh, dear God, dear God. . . ."

"Nastenka," I cried, unable to restrain myself any longer, "this is more than I can endure! It's sheer torture to me! You wound me to the heart, Nastenka! I can't be silent! I must speak! I must tell you of all the anguish in my heart!"

Saying this, I raised myself from the seat. She took my hand and looked at me in surprise.

"What's the matter?" she said at last.

"Listen to me, Nastenka," I said firmly, "listen to me, please! What I'm going to say to you now is all nonsense. It is foolish. It cannot be. I know it will never happen, but I cannot remain silent. In the name of all that you're suffering now, I beseech you beforehand to forgive me!"

"Well, what is it? What is it?" she demanded, and she stopped crying and looked intently at me, a strange gleam of curiosity in her startled eyes. "What is the matter with you?"

"It's out of the question, I know, but—I love you, Nastenka! That is what's the matter with me. Now you know everything!" I said, with a despairing wave of my hand. "Now you can judge for yourself whether you ought to go on talking to me as you did just now, and—what is perhaps even more important— whether you ought to listen to what I'm going to say to you."

"Well, what about it?" Nastenka interrupted. "Of course I knew long ago that you loved me, only I always thought that— well, that you loved me in the ordinary way, I mean that you were just fond of me. Oh dear, oh dear! . . ."

"At first it was in the ordinary way, Nastenka, but now— now I'm in the same position as you were when you went to him with your bundle that night. I'm in a worse position Nastenka, because he wasn't in love with anyone at the time, and you—you are."

"Goodness, what are you saying to me! I really can't understand you. But, look, what has made you—I mean, why did you—and so suddenly too! Oh dear, I'm talking such nonsense! But you——"

And Nastenka got completely confused. Her cheeks were flushed. She dropped her eyes.

"What's to be done, Nastenka? What can I do about it? It's entirely my fault, of course. I've taken an unfair advantage of— But no—no, Nastenka, it isn't my fault. I know it isn't. I feel it isn't because my heart tells me I'm right, because I could never do anything to hurt you, because I could do nothing that you would ever take offence at. I was your friend? Well, I still am your friend. I have not been unfaithful to anyone. You see, I'm crying, Nastenka. But never mind. What if tears do run down my cheeks? Let them. They don't hurt anyone. They'll soon dry, Nastenka."

"But sit down, do sit down, please," she said, making me sit down on the seat. "Oh dear, oh dear!"

"No, Nastenka, I shan't sit down. I can't stay here any longer. You'll never see me again. I'll say what I have to say and go away. I only want to say that you'd never have found out that I loved you. I'd never have told my secret to a living soul. I'd never have tormented you with my egoism at such a moment. Never! But I could not bear to be silent now. It was you who began talking about it. It's your fault, not mine. You just can't drive me away from you."

"But I'm not—I'm not driving you away from me!" Nastenka said, doing her best, poor child, not to show how embarrassed she was.

"You are not driving me away? No—but I meant to run away from you myself. And I will go away. I will. Only first let me tell you everything, for, you see, when you were talking to me here,

I couldn't sit still; when you cried here, when you tormented yourself because—well, because (I'd better say it, Nastenka)—because you were jilted, because your love was slighted and disregarded, I felt that in my heart there was so much love for you, Nastenka, so much love! And I so bitterly resented not being able to do anything to help you with my love that—that my heart was bursting and I—I couldn't be silent any longer, Nastenka. I had to speak!"

"Yes, yes, tell me everything, do speak to me like that!" said Nastenka with a gesture that touched me deeply. "It may seem strange to you that I should be speaking to you like this, but—do say what you have to say! I will tell you afterwards. I'll tell you everything!"

"You are sorry for me, Nastenka. You're just sorry for me, my dear, dear friend! Well, what's done is done. No use crying over spilt milk, is it? Well, so you know everything now. At any rate, that's something to start with. All right. Everything's fine now. Only, please, listen. When you were sitting here, when you were crying, I thought to myself (Oh, do let me tell you what I was thinking!), I thought that (I know of course how utterly impossible it is, Nastenka)—I thought that you—that you somehow—I mean quite apart from anything else—that you no longer cared for him. If that is so, then—I already thought of that yesterday, Nastenka, and the day before yesterday—then I would—I most certainly would have done my best to make you care for me. You said yourself, Nastenka—you did say it several times, didn't you?—that you almost loved me. Well, what more is there to tell you? That's really all I wanted to say. All that remains to be said is what would happen if you fell in love with me—that's all—nothing more! Now listen to me, my friend—for you are my friend, aren't you?—I am of course an ordinary sort of fellow, poor and insignificant, but that doesn't matter (I'm afraid I don't seem to be putting it very well, Nastenka, because I'm so confused), what matters is that I'd love you so well, so well, Nastenka, that even if you still loved him and went on loving the man I don't know, my love would never be a burden to you. All you'd feel, all you'd be conscious of every minute, is that a very grateful heart was beating at your side, Nastenka, an ardent heart which for your sake—Oh, Nastenka, Nastenka, what have you done to me?"

"Don't cry, I don't want you to cry," said Nastenka, rising quickly from the seat. "Come along, get up, come with me. Don't cry, don't cry," she said, drying my tears with her handkerchief. "There, come along now. Perhaps I'll tell you something. Well, if he has really given me up, if he has forgotten me, then though I still love him (and I don't want to deceive you)— But, listen, answer me! If, for instance, I were to fall in love with you—I mean, if only I—Oh, my friend, my friend, when I think, when I only think how I must have offended you when I laughed at your love, when I praised you for not falling in love with me! Oh dear, why didn't I foresee it? Why didn't I foresee it? How could I have been so stupid? But never mind, I've made up my mind now. I'm going to tell you everything."

"Look here, Nastenka, do you know what? I'll go away. Yes, I'll go away! I can see that I'm simply tormenting you. Now you're sorry you've been making fun of me, and I hate to think—yes, I simply hate to think that in addition to your own sorrow—Of course, it's all my fault, Nastenka, it's all my fault, but—goodbye!"

"Stop! Listen to me first, please. You can wait, can't you?"

"Wait? What should I wait for? What do you mean?"

"You see, I love him, but that will pass. It must pass. It's quite impossible for it not to pass. As a matter of fact, it's already passing. I can feel it. Who knows, maybe it'll be over today, for I hate him! Yes, I hate him because he has slighted me, while you were weeping with me. I hate him because you haven't let me down as he has, because you love me, while he has never really loved me, because—well, because I love you too. Yes, I love you! I love you as you love me. I've told you so before, haven't I? You heard me say it yourself. I love you because you're better than he is, because you're more honourable than he is, because he—"

She stopped crying at last, dried her eyes, and we continued our walk. I wanted to say something, but she kept asking me to wait. We were silent. At last she plucked up courage and began to speak.

"Look," she said, in a weak and trembling voice, in which, however, there was a strange note which pierced my heart and filled it with a sweet sensation of joy, "don't think I'm so fickle, so inconstant. Don't think that I can forget him so easily and so quickly, that I can be untrue to him. I have loved him for a whole year, and I swear I have never, never for a moment, been untrue to him even in thought. He has thought little of that, he has scorned me—well, I don't mind that. But he has also hurt my feelings and wrung my heart. I don't love him because I can only love what is generous, what is understanding, what is honourable, for I'm like that myself, and he's not worthy of me. Well, let's forget about him. I'd rather he behaved to me like that now than that I was disappointed later in my expectations and found out the sort of man he really was. Anyway, it's all over now. And, besides, my dear friend," she went on, pressing my hand, "who knows, perhaps my love for him was nothing but self-deception, nothing but imagination. Perhaps it started just as a joke, just as a bit of silly nonsense because I was constantly under Granny's supervision. Perhaps I ought to love another man and not him, quite a different man, a man who'd have pity on me, and—and—anyway," Nastenka broke off, overcome with emotion, "don't let's speak of it. Don't let's speak of it. I only wanted to tell you—I wanted to tell you that even if I do love him (no, did love him), even if in spite of this you still say—or rather feel that your love is so great that it could in time replace my love for him in my heart—if you really and truly have pity on me, if you won't leave me alone to my fate, without consolation, without hope, if you promise to love me always as you love me now, then I swear that my gratitude—that my love will in time be worthy of your love. Will you take my hand now?"

"Nastenka," I cried, my voice broken with sobs, "Nastenka! Oh, Nastenka!"

"All right, all right!" she said, making a great effort to speak calmly. "All right! That's enough! Now everything's been said, hasn't it? Hasn't it? Well, you are happy now, aren't you? And I too am happy. So don't let's talk about it any more. Just wait a little—have patience—spare me! Talk of something else, for God's sake!"

"Yes, Nastenka, yes! Of course don't let's talk about it. Now I'm happy. Well, Nastenka, do let's talk of something else. Come on, let's. I don't mind."

But we did not know what to talk about. We laughed, we cried, we said a thousand things without caring whether they made sense or not. One moment we walked along the pavement, and the next we suddenly turned back and crossed the road, then we stopped and crossed over to the embankment again. We were like children. . . .

"I'm living alone, now, Nastenka," I began, "but tomorrow——You know, of course, Nastenka, that I'm poor, don't you? I've only got twelve hundred roubles, but that doesn't matter."

"Of course not, and Granny has her pension, so that she won't be a burden to us. We'll have to take Granny, of course."

"Of course we'll take Granny! Only—there's Matryona——"

"Goodness, I never thought of that! And we've got Fyokla!"

"Matryona is a good soul, only she has one fault: she has no imagination, Nastenka, none whatever! But I don't suppose that matters!"

"It makes no difference. They can live together. You'll move to our house tomorrow, won't you?"

"How do you mean? To your house? Oh, very well, I don't mind."

"I mean, you'll take our attic. I told you we have an attic, didn't I? It's empty now. We had a woman lodger, an old gentlewoman, but she's left, and I know Granny would like to let it to a young man. I said to her, 'Why a young man, Granny?' But she said, 'Why not? I'm old and I like young people about. You don't think I'm trying to get a husband for you, do you?' Well, I saw at once of course that that was what she had in mind."

"Good Lord, Nastenka!"

And we both laughed.

"Oh, well, never mind. But where do you live? I've forgotten."

I told her I lived near a certain bridge in Barannikov's house.

"It's a very big house, isn't it?"

"Yes, it's a very big house."

"Oh, yes, I know it. It's a nice house, but I still think you ought to move out of it and come and live with us as soon as possible."

"I'll do so tomorrow, Nastenka, tomorrow. I'm afraid I'm a little behindhand with my rent, but that doesn't matter. I shall be getting my salary soon and—"

"And you know I could be giving lessons. Yes, why not? I'll learn everything myself first and then give lessons."

"That's an excellent idea, Nastenka, an excellent idea! And I'll be getting a bonus soon. . . ."

"So tomorrow you'll be my lodger. . . ."

"Yes, and we'll go to *The Barber of Seville*, for I believe they're going to put it on again soon."

"Oh yes, I'd love to," said Nastenka, laughing. "Perhaps not *The Barber*, though. We'd better see something else."

"Oh, all right, something else then. I don't mind. I suppose something else would be better. You see, I didn't think—"

Talking like this, we walked along in a sort of a daze, in a mist, as though we did not know ourselves what was happening to us. One moment we would stop and go on talking in one place for a long time, and the next we would be walking again till we would find ourselves goodness knows where—and more laughter, more tears. Then Nastenka would suddenly decide that she ought to be going back home, and I would not dare to detain her, but would insist on accompanying her to her house. We would start on our way back, and in about a quarter of an hour would find ourselves on the embankment by our seat. Then she would sigh, and tears would come into her eyes again, and I would be plunged into despair and a chilly premonition of disaster would steal into my heart. But she would at once press my hand and drag me off again to walk, talk, chatter. . . .

"It's time—time I went home now," Nastenka said at last. "I think it must be awfully late. We've been behaving like children long enough!"

"Yes, of course, Nastenka. Only I don't suppose I shall be able to sleep now. No, I won't go home."

"I don't think I shall sleep, either. Only see me home, will you?"

"Of course, I'll see you home. . . ."

"On your word of honour? Because, you see, I must get back home some time, mustn't I?"

"On my word of honour!" I replied, laughing.

"All right, let's go."

"Let's go. Look at the sky, Nastenka, look! It'll be a lovely day tomorrow! What a blue sky! What a moon! Look, a yellow cloud is drifting over it. Look! Look! No, it has passed by. Look, Nastenka, look!"

But Nastenka did not look. She stood speechless, motionless. A minute later she clung somewhat timidly close to me. Her hand trembled in mine. I looked at her. She clung to me more closely.

At that moment a young man passed by us. He suddenly stopped, looked at us intently for a moment, and then again took a few steps towards us. My heart missed a beat.

"Nastenka," I said in an undertone, "who is it Nastenka?"

"It's him!" she replied in a whisper, clinging to me still more closely, still more tremulously.

I could hardly stand up.

"Nastenka! Nastenka! It's you!" we heard a voice behind us, and at the same time the young man took a few steps towards us.

Lord, how she cried out! How she started! How she tore herself out of my hands and rushed to meet him! I stood and looked at them, utterly crushed. But no sooner had she given him her hand, no sooner had she thrown herself into his arms, than she suddenly turned to me again, and was at my side in a flash, faster than lightning, faster than the wind, and before I could recover from my surprise, flung her arms round my neck and kissed me ardently. Then, without uttering a word, she rushed back to him again, clasped his hands, and drew him after her.

I stood a long time, watching them walking away. At last both of them vanished from my sight.

Morning

My nights came to an end with a morning. The weather was dreadful. It was pouring, and the rain kept beating dismally against my windowpanes. It was dark in the room; it was dull and dreary outside. My head ached. I felt giddy. I was beginning to feel feverish.

"A letter for you, sir," said Matryona, bending over me. "Came by the city post, it did, sir. The postman brought it."

"A letter? Who from?" I cried, jumping up from my chair.

"I don't know, sir, I'm sure. I suppose whoever sent it must have signed his name."

I broke the seal: the letter was from her!

"Oh, forgive me, forgive me!" Nastenka wrote to me. "I beg you on my knees to forgive me! I deceived you and myself. It was all a dream, a delusion. I nearly died today thinking of you. Please, please forgive me!

"Don't blame me, for I haven't changed a bit towards you. I said I would love you, and I do love you now, I more than love you. Oh, if only I could love both of you at once! Oh, if only you were he!"

"Oh, if only he were you!" it flashed through my mind. "Those were your own words, Nastenka!"

"God knows what I would do for you now. I know how sad and unhappy you must be. I've treated you abominably, but when one loves, you know, an injury is soon forgotten. And you do love me!

"Thank you, yes! thank you for that love. For it remains imprinted in my memory like a sweet dream one remembers a long time after awakening. I shall never forget the moment when you opened your heart to me like a real friend, when you accepted the gift of my broken heart to take care of it, to cherish it, to heal it. If you forgive me, I promise you that the memory of you will always remain with me, that I shall be everlastingly grateful to you, and that my feeling of gratitude will never be erased from my heart. I shall treasure this memory, I'll be true to it. I shall never be unfaithful to it, I shall never be unfaithful to my heart. It is too constant for that. It returned so quickly yesterday to him to whom it has always belonged.

"We shall meet. You will come and see us. You will not leave us, will you? You'll always be my friend, my brother. And when you see me, you'll give me your hand, won't you? You will give it to me because you've forgiven me. You have, haven't you? You love me *as before*, don't you?

"Oh, yes, do love me! Don't ever forsake me, because I love you so at this moment, because I am worthy of your love, because I promise to deserve it—oh, my dear, dear friend! Next week I'm to be married to him. He has come back as much in love with me as ever. He has never forgotten me. You will not be angry with me because I have written about him, will you? I would like to come and see you with him. You will like him, won't you?

"Forgive me, remember and love your Nastenka."

I read this letter over and over again. There were tears in my eyes. At last it dropped out of my hands, and I buried my face.

"Look, love, look!" Matryona called me.

"What is it, Matryona?"

"Why, I've swept all the cobwebs off the ceiling. Looks so lovely and clean, you could be wed, love, and have your wedding party here. You might just as well do it now as wait till it gets dirty again!"

I looked at Matryona. She was still hale and hearty, quite a *young-looking* old woman, in fact. But I don't know why all of a sudden she looked old and decrepit to me, with a wrinkled face and lustreless eyes. I don't know why, but all of a sudden my room, too, seemed to have grown as old as Matryona. The walls and floors looked discoloured, everything was dark and grimy, and the cobwebs were thicker than ever. I don't know why, but when I looked out of the window the house opposite, too, looked dilapidated and dingy, the plaster on its columns peeling and crumbling, its cornices blackened and full of cracks, and its bright brown walls disfigured by large white and yellow patches. Either the sun, appearing suddenly from behind the dark rain-clouds, had hidden itself so quickly that everything had grown dark before my eyes again, or perhaps the whole sombre and melancholy perspective of my future flashed before my mind's eye at that moment, and I saw myself just as I was now fifteen years hence, only grown older, in the same room, living the same sort of solitary life, with the same Matryona, who had not grown a bit wiser in all those years.

But that I should feel any resentment against you, Nastenka! That I should cast a dark shadow over your bright, serene happiness! That I should chill and darken your heart with bitter reproaches, wound it with secret remorse, cause it to beat anxiously at the moment of bliss! That I should crush a single one of those delicate blooms which you will wear in your dark hair when you walk up the aisle to the altar with him! Oh no— never, never! May your sky be always clear, may your dear smile be always bright and happy, and may you be for ever blessed for that moment of bliss and happiness which you gave to another lonely and grateful heart!

Good Lord, only a *moment* of bliss? Isn't such a moment sufficient for the whole of a man's life?

A DISGRACEFUL AFFAIR

TRANSLATED BY NORA GOTTLIEB

Our beloved motherland was experiencing a renaissance; her brave sons, fired with impulses at once touching and naïve, were seeking with an uncontrollable yearning for new destinies and hopes. It was at this time that the following disgraceful affair took place.

to now. The celebration was nothing very much; as we have already seen, there were only two guests, both former colleagues and subordinates of Mr. Nikiforov's, namely: one, Actual State Councillor Semyon Ivanovitch Shipulenko; and the other, also Actual State Councillor, Ivan Ilyitch Pralinski. They had come to take tea around nine o'clock and had afterwards tackled some wine, and they knew that they would have to leave promptly at half past eleven. Their host had all his life had a liking for regular habits. Let me say two words about him: he had begun his career as an impecunious petty Government official, gently spinning it out for forty-five years, knowing too well how far he could hope to rise. He could not bear to snatch at the stars above (although he already wore two of them on his tunic) and in particular he disliked expressing his own personal views on any matter whatever. He was honest, too; or rather, he had never had occasion to be particularly dishonest; an egoist, he was single; he was no fool, but disliked parading his intellect. He could not stand disorder and enthusiasm, which he considered a sort of moral untidiness, and by the end of his life he was submerged in a kind of sweet, indolent comfort and well-ordered solitariness. Although he himself had sometimes visited his superiors, even as a young man he had been unable to endure receiving guests, and lately, when he was not playing Grand Patience, he had contented himself with the company of his dining-room clock. Drowsing in an arm-chair, he would listen placidly for whole evenings to it ticking on the mantelpiece beneath its glass case. In appearance he was very respectable; clean-shaven, he looked younger than his years; he was well preserved, showed signs of living for a long while yet, and conformed to the highest standards of gentlemanly behaviour.

The position he held was comfortable enough: he sat on a Board and signed something or other.

In brief, he was considered a most worthy person.

He had only one passion, or better, one ardent desire: that was to possess his own house, and in particular a house built in the style of a gentleman's residence, not a tenement for letting at a profit. At last this wish had been realized. He had looked round and bought a house on the Petersburg Side; true, it was rather far out, but it was an elegant residence, and, moreover, it had a garden. The new owner maintained it was even better for being farther out; he did not like entertaining at home, and for visiting anyone or driving to the office, he had a fine chocolate-coloured two-seater carriage, a coachman called Mikhei and a pair of small but strong, handsome horses. All this was the fruit of forty years' painstaking economy, and his heart rejoiced in it.

Hence, when he had bought the house and moved in, Stepan Nikiforovitch was overcome by such contentment that in the serenity of his heart he actually invited guests on his birthday, which formerly he had carefully kept from even his closest friends.

He had, however, an ulterior motive in inviting one of his guests. He himself occupied the upper floor of his house, while the ground floor, which was set out in exactly the same way, required a tenant. And so Stepan Nikiforovitch looked to Semyon Ivanovitch Shipulenko, and in the course of the evening had twice steered the conversation towards this objective. But Semyon Ivanovitch was non-committal. Here was a man who had also made his way painstakingly and over a long period; he had black hair and whiskers and a jaundiced countenance. Married, a surly stay-at-home, he tyrannized his household; he performed his duties with self-confidence, and he, too, was well aware of his capabilities and, better still, of what he would never achieve; he was sitting pretty in a comfortable job, and sitting tight. He looked on the new order of things not entirely without rancour, yet was not unduly concerned. He was very sure of himself and it was not without malicious scorn that he listened to the ramblings of Ivan Ilyitch Pralinski on topics of the day. As a matter of fact, they had all had a little too much to drink, so that even Stepan Nikiforovitch condescended to launch forth in a slight argument with Mr. Pralinski on the subject of the new reforms. But a few words must be mentioned about His Excellency Mr. Pralinski, particularly as he is, in fact, the chief hero of our story.

Only four months had passed since State Councillor Ivan Ilyitch Pralinski had begun to be addressed as "Your Excellency"; in fact he was a newly created General. And he was still young in years, about forty-three, certainly not more and looked, and liked to look, younger. He was a handsome man, tall, and clothes-conscious; he had the proper knack of wearing a distinguished order round his neck. From childhood he had learned to adopt some habits of the fashionable world, and, as a bachelor, he dreamed of a rich bride, even a bride from high society. There were many other things he dreamed of, though he was far from stupid. At times he was a great talker, and even liked to adopt the airs of a parliamentarian. He was of good family, the pampered son of a General, and at a tender age was clothed in velvet and fine linen; he had been educated in an aristocratic establishment, and although he had gained little learning therein he had succeeded in office and managed to rise to the rank of General. His superiors regarded him as a gifted person and had great hopes for him. Stepan Nikiforovitch, under whom he had begun and continued his office career almost up to the time when he rose to the rank of a General, had never considered him very businesslike and had no hope whatsoever for him. But it pleased him that he was of good family, had private means—that is, he owned a large and profitable house, with its own caretaker—was related to folk of good standing and, above all, had a certain air of distinction about him. Stepan Nikiforovitch secretly reproached him for his excess of imagination and frivolity. Ivan Ilyitch himself sometimes felt that he was too vain and even over-sensitive. It was a queer thing: at times he had attacks of morbid conscience and even a slight feeling of remorse. With bitterness and secret heartache he admitted to himself that he did not really fly as high as he liked to think. At these moments he felt dejected, especially when his attack of piles was at its worst, and called his life "*une existence manquée*", lost faith (privately, of course) even in his debating abilities, referring to himself as an empty talker and a phrasemonger. Although all this was certainly much to his credit, it did not in the least impede his spirits from rising half an hour later, when he would more obstinately and more presumptuously than ever reassure and convince himself that he still had time to prove his worth and would not only reach a high rank but would moreover become a great statesman, long to be remembered in Russia. At times he even visualized pecially as Semyon Ivanovitch Shipulenko, whom he particularly despised and feared for his cynicism and spitefulness, sat beside him in crafty silence, smiling more often than was necessary. "They appear to me taking me for a puppy!" the thought flashed through Ivan Ilyitch's mind.

"No, sir it's time, it was time long ago," he continued hotly. "We have talked too long and it is my opinion that the chief thing is to be humane, to be considerate towards one's inferiors, bearing in mind that they too are human beings. Idealism will save all, will be the universal panacea. . . ."

"He-he-he!" chuckled Semyon Ivanovitch from his corner.

"But why are you reproaching us?" finally objected Stepan Nikiforovitch with an amiable smile. "I must confess, Ivan Ilyitch, I have not yet been able to grasp what you are so kindly explaining to us. You are extolling idealism. That means love of mankind, doesn't it?"

"Yes, perhaps, granted, call it love of mankind. I . . ."

"Permit me, sir! As far as I can judge, that is not the whole point. There was always a need for love of mankind; the Reform Act does not stop at that. Various problems have arisen relating to the peasantry, the law, agriculture, the payment of compensation, morals and . . . there is no end to these problems, and all in all, united, they could cause, so to speak, great upheavals. That was what we feared, not merely some sort of idealism . . ."

"Yes, sir, the matter is rather more involved," remarked Semyon Ivanovitch.

"I understand very well, sir, and permit me to remark, Semyon Ivanovitch, that I am in no way ready to lag behind you in comprehending the depths of the problem," remarked Ivan

Ilyitch caustically, "but, nevertheless, I'll venture to remark to you, Stepan Nikoforovitch as well, that you too have not understood me at all. . . ."

"Indeed, I have not."

"Yes, I expressly continue to uphold and I attempt to spread the idea that idealism, consideration, particularly towards one's inferiors, from official to clerk, clerk to house-servant, house-servant to peasant—idealism, I say, could serve as the keystone to the impending reforms and, on the whole, to the regeneration of every facet of life. Why? This is why: take the following syllogism: I am humane, consequently I am loved. They love me, then presumably they trust me. They put their trust in me, consequently they believe in me, therefore love me . . . that is, no, I mean to say, if they believe, they will also believe in reform, they will understand, so to speak, the very heart of the matter. They will, so to speak, morally embrace one another, and will settle everything fundamentally in a friendly spirit. What are you giggling about, Semyon Ivanovitch? Don't you follow?"

Stepan Nikiforovitch raised his brows in silence; he was astonished.

"It seems to me I've had a drop too much," remarked Semyon Ivanovitch maliciously, "and therefore I am a little slow on the uptake. A kind of mental blackout, sir."

Ivan Ilyitch winced.

"We shan't live up to it," Stepan Nikiforovitch suddenly pronounced on brief reflection.

"What's that? We shan't live up to it?" asked Ivan Ilyitch, surprised at this sudden and abrupt remark coming from Stepan Nikiforovitch.

"Just that: we shan't live up to it." Stepan Nikiforovitch evidently did not want to enlarge on his remark.

"Are you referring to 'new wine in old bottles'?" retorted Ivan Ilyitch, not without irony. "Oh no, sir, I am sure I can vouch for myself."

At that moment the clock struck half past eleven.

"Here we sit like birds in a desert," said Semyon Ivanovitch, preparing to rise. But Ivan Ilyitch forestalled him, immediately getting up and taking his sable hat from the mantelpiece. He looked hurt.

"What about it, Semyon Ivanovitch, will you think it over?" said Stepan Nikiforovitch, seeing his guests off.

"About the flat? I'll think it over. Yes, I'll think it over."

"And let me have your decision quickly?"

"Still talking business?" remarked Mr. Pralinski ingratiatingly, playing with his hat. It seemed to him as though he was being left out.

Stepan Nikiforovitch raised his eyebrows and remained silent, as a sign that he was not detaining his guests. Semyon Ivanovitch hurriedly took his leave.

"Ah . . . well . . . have it your own way! If you don't understand common courtesy," decided Mr. Pralinski, and with a particularly conscious air of independence he held out his hand to Stepan Nikiforovitch.

In the hall Ivan Ilyitch wrapped himself in his light and expensive fur coat, trying not to notice Semyon Ivanovitch's wellworn raccoon and they both began to descend the stairs.

"It seems our old man is offended," said Ivan Ilyitch to the silent Semyon Ivanovitch.

"Not in the least," answered the other calmly and coldly.

"Serf mentality!" thought Ivan Ilyitch.

When they had stepped down from the porch, Semyon Ivanovitch's sledge was brought up, with its plain grey nag.

"What the devil! What has Trifon done with my carriage?" cried Ivan Ilyitch, not seeing it.

He glanced hither and thither, but there was no carriage in sight. Stepan Nikiforovitch's servant had no idea of its where-abouts. They inquired of Varlam, Semyon Ivanovitch's coach-man and were told Trifon had been around the whole time, the carriage as well, but now they were gone.

"Disgraceful!" put in Mr. Shipulenko. "Would you like a lift?"

"What wretches these people are!" cried Mr. Pralinski in a rage. "He asked me, the scoundrel, to let him off for a wedding somewhere here on the Petersburg Side, some sort of relative was to be married, the devil take her. I strictly forbade him to abandon his post. And now I'll bet he has gone there."

"That's actually what he has done," remarked Varlam. "He went there, but promised to be back in a jiffy; that is, to be back just in time."

"So that's it! I somehow felt this would happen. You wait; he'll catch it."

"You'd better have him thrashed twice at the police station; that will make him carry out your orders better," said Semyon Ivanovitch, drawing the fur cover of the sledge over himself.

"Please don't worry, Semyon Ivanovitch."

"So you don't want a lift home?"

"No, *merci*. A pleasant journey."

Semyon Ivanovitch drove away, while Ivan Ilyitch, feeling intensely irritated, set off walking along the wooden causeway.

———————————————

"I'll show you now, you rogue! I'll walk home on purpose, just to make you realize, just to frighten you! You'll return and find out that the master has had to go off on foot . . . good-for-nothing!"

Never before had Ivan Ilyitch sworn so at anyone, but he was in an excessive rage, and on top of this his head was humming. He was unaccustomed to drink, which is why some five or six glasses of champagne quickly affected him. However, the night was enchanting. It was frosty but unusually silent and still. The sky was clear and full of stars. The full moon shed her pale silvery light over the earth. It was so lovely that having gone about fifty paces Ivan Ilyitch almost forgot his misfortune. He began feeling particularly contented. People in a state of intoxication are prone, in any case, to quick changes of mood. He even began to like the unsightly little wooden houses of the empty street.

"It's a good thing, after all, that I've had to walk," he thought. "It's a lesson to Trifon and a pleasure for me. I really ought to take walks more often. It won't do me any harm. I shall find a cab at once on the Bolshoi Prospect. What a lovely night! What odd little houses these are! Probably small folk live here—petty officials . . . shopkeepers maybe. . . . That queer Stepan Nikiforovitch! What reactionaries they all are! Wet blankets. Wet blankets, that's precisely what they are, *c'est le mot*. . . . He is a clever man, though: he has this *bon sens*, a sober, practical understanding of things. But in spite of this they are real old men! They lack the—what could one call it? Well, they lack something. . . . We shan't live up to it! What did he mean by that? He even became thoughtful when he said it. . . . Incidentally, he never understood me at all. And how could he fail to understand? It was more difficult not to understand than to understand. The main thing is that I am convinced, convinced in my innermost heart. Idealism—love for mankind! To restore man to himself. . . . To restore him his self-respect and then—with such material in hand, set to work. It seems clear enough! Yes, sir. Just permit me this, Your Excellency; take the following syllogism: we meet, for instance, a petty clerk, a poor, downtrodden clerk. Well . . . and who are you? The answer is: a clerk. Very well, a clerk; more: what kind of clerk? The answer is: such and such a clerk, he says. Are you working? Yes, I am working! Do you want to be happy? I do. What do you need to make you happy? This and that. Why? Because . . . And here you have a man who understands me at once, the man is mine, caught, so to speak, in my nets, and I can do anything I like with him. That is, for his own good. Disgraceful man, that Semyon Ivanovitch! and what a nasty mug he has. To have Trifon whipped at the police station—he said that deliberately. No, you're wrong, whip him yourself; I am not in favour of whipping, I'll put Trifon in his place with words, with a rebuke, that will make him realize. As for using the whip, h'm . . . that question is as yet unsolved, h'm. . . . Shall I look in at Emerance's? Ugh! The devil take these damned pavements!" he cried out as he tripped up on something. "And this is the capital. This is supposed to be civilization! You might break your leg. H'm. . . . I cannot stand that Semyon Ivanovitch, a most unpleasant mug. He was sniggering at me when I talked about 'moral embrace'. Well, and if they embrace, what's that got to do with you? Don't worry, I won't embrace you; rather embrace a peasant. . . . If I come across a peasant, well, I'll talk to him. However, I was drunk and perhaps did not express myself quite clearly. Even now, perhaps, I'm not expressing myself properly. . . . H'm. . . . I'll never get drunk again. In the evening you talk freely and next day you regret it. I am not swaying on my feet, am I? Ah well, they are all scoundrels, just the same!"

So, at random, Ivan Ilyitch, conducted an incoherent discussion with himself as he continued to walk along the pavement. The fresh air was having its effect on him and had, you might say, sobered him. Five minutes later he would have calmed down and felt sleepy. But suddenly, within a couple of paces of the Bolshoi Prospect, he thought he heard the sound of music. He looked round. On the other side of the street, in a very ramshackle wooden house, one-storied but long, a party seemed to be in full swing; the fiddles hooted, the double-bass creaked and the flute sang shrilly to the tempo of a gay quadrille. A crowd had gathered below the windows, mostly of women in quilted coats and shawls over their heads; they were trying their best to see between the chinks of the shutters what was going on. Apparently all was gaiety within. The thump of the dancers' feet could be heard across the street. Ivan Ilyitch noticed a policeman near by and approached him.

"Whose house is it, old fellow?" he asked, throwing open his expensive fur-lined coat a little, just enough to let the policeman see the important decoration he was wearing.

"It is Pseldonymov's; he is a clerk, a registrar," answered the policeman, straightening himself as he caught a glimpse of the medal.

"Pseldonymov's! I never! What about him! Is he getting married?"

"He is, Your Honour, to the daughter of a Titular Councillor. Mlekopitayev, Titular Councillor he is . . . the one who used to work in the City Council. This house goes with the bride."

"So that is now Pseldonymov's and not Mlekopitayev's house?"

"It is Pseldonymov's, Your Honour. It used to be Mlekopitayev's before, but now it is Pseldonymov's."

"H'm. I am asking you this, my good man, because I am his chief. I am the General in charge of the very office in which Pseldonymov works."

"Quite so, Your Excellency," said the policeman, finally drawing himself up to his full height, while Ivan Ilyitch appeared to grow pensive. He stood there, thinking. . . .

Yes, indeed, Pseldonymov was in his department, even in his own office; he did remember that. He was a very junior official with a salary of some ten roubles a month. As Mr. Pralinski had only very recently taken over his department, he did not remember all his underlings too well, but Pseldonymov he did remember, just because of his name. It had immediately caught his eye, so that he had been curious enough to look more closely at the owner of so strange a name. He now remembered a very young man with a long hooked nose and colourless bristly hair; he was anaemic and underfed, and wore an impossible uniform and impossible, even indecent, nether garments. He remembered that at the time the thought had crossed his mind: ought he not to give the poor devil a bonus of ten roubles for the New Year to rig himself out? But because the poor fellow wore an over-hypocritical expression on his face and because his appearance was extremely unattractive, even to the point of repulsion, the kind thought had somehow evaporated, so that in the end Pseldonymov had remained without bonus. He was all the more surprised when, a week earlier, this same Pseldonymov had approached him with the request to get married. Ivan Ilyitch remembered that at the time he had been too busy to take the matter up properly, so that the question of the marriage was decided casually and hurriedly. Nevertheless, he distinctly remembered that his bride was bringing Pseldonymov a wooden house and a clear four hundred roubles; this fact had astonished him at the time; he remembered he had even made a pun about the combination of the surnames Pseldonymov and Mlekopitayev. All this he clearly recalled.

As he remembered he became more and more lost in reflection. It is well known that a whole train of thought can pass through one's mind in a flash in the form of some kind of feeling, without being translated into human language, let alone into writing. However, we shall try to convey all the feelings of our hero and bring before the reader at least something of their substance, so to speak, everything that was most essential and most plausible in them. Because many of our feelings, put into ordinary words, would appear quite implausible, would they not? That is why they are never revealed, but remain locked up within us. Of course, Ivan Ilyitch's feelings and thoughts were a little incoherent. But then you know the reason for this.

"Now, why," passed through his mind, "is it that we all indulge in talk, but when it comes to action nothing comes of it but a mockery? For instance, take that self-same Pseldonymov: he

came back from the wedding ceremony a short while ago, all
excited, full of hope, ready to taste joy . . . this is one of the
most blissful days of his life. Now he is fussing around with
his guests, giving a party—a modest, meagre party, but all the
same a happy and genuine one. . . . What would happen if he
realized that at this very moment I—I—his most exalted di-
rector, am standing by his house and listening to his music?
Indeed, what would he do? But really! what would he do, if
I suddenly took it into my head to go in? H'm . . . naturally,
he would at first take fright, struck dumb with confusion. I
should disturb him, spoil everything, perhaps . . . yes, this
would happen, if any other General intruded, but not with
me. . . . That's the point, with any other, but assuredly not
with me. . . .

"Yes, Stepan Nikiforovitch! You refused to understand me a
short while ago, but here you have a living example. Yes, sir. We
are all shouting about humanitarianism, but are incapable of
herosim, of a heroic act.

"What heroism? Why, this! Just consider: despite the way all
members of society feel about each other, here I myself shall
turn up at one o'clock in the morning at the wedding of my
underling, a registrar, earning ten roubles a month; but this is
madness, this would create havoc, wouldn't it turn things up-
side down, the last day of Pompeii, utter chaos? Nobody would
understand it. Stepan Nikiforovitch wouldn't understand it to
his dying day. Didn't he say: we shan't live up to it? But that re-
fers to you old men, paralyzed and stagnating, whereas I shall!
I'll transform the last day of Pompeii into the sweetest day for
my clerk, and an eccentric act into a normal, patriarchal, lofty
and moral gesture. How? Like this. Kindly listen:

"Well . . . let's suppose that I go in: they are astonished, break off dancing, draw back, overawed. Yes, but it is here that I reveal my quality: I march straight up to the frightened Pseldonymov and say with the most affectionate smile, in the simplest words: 'It's like this,' I say. I have been visiting His Excellency Stepan Nikiforovitch. I expect you know him, a neighbour of yours. . . ." And then, in a slightly comic tone, I recount the incident with Trifon. From Trifon I pass on to the fact that I had to walk. . . . Well, then—that I heard music, asked of the policeman what the noise was and learned that you, my friend, had just got married. I'll go to my underling's house, think I; I'll see how my clerks enjoy themselves and how they get married. I don't suppose you'd show me the door, would you? Turn me out! What an expression in the mouth of one's underling. What the devil—turn me out indeed; I think he would more likely lose his head, rush to settle me in an arm-chair, tremble with delight, at first quite distracted.

"Now what could be simpler, more gracious than such an action? Why did I go in? That is another question. That is, so to speak, the moral aspect of the matter. That is the core of the matter.

"H'm . . . oh dear me, what was I thinking about? Oh yes.

"And naturally they will put me next to the most important guest, some sort of Titular Councillor or relative, a retired staff-captain with a red nose . . . how well Gogol described these characters! And, of course, I am introduced to the bride. I compliment her, I encourage the guests. I ask them to be at their ease, to go on enjoying themselves, continue dancing; I play the wit, I laugh—in short, I am amiable and charming. After all, I always am amiable and charming when I am pleased with myself. . . . H'm . . . the truth is, I'm still, it seems, not exactly drunk, but somewhat . . .

" . . . Of course, being a gentleman I shall treat them as equals and on no account demand any special attention. . . . But from the moral point of view . . . this is another matter: they will understand and appreciate me properly . . . my action will revive in them a sense of their own dignity. . . . Well, I stay there, for half an hour . . . maybe even a whole hour. It is obvious that I leave just before supper. They will start bustling, start baking and roasting, they will bow low before me, but I shall just drink to the health of the newly-weds and decline to take supper. I shall say: 'I have some business to attend to', and as soon as I say the word 'business' everyone's face will assume a respectful and serious expression. In this way I shall tactfully remind them that between myself and them there is a difference. . . . Like heaven and earth. Not that I mean to suggest that, but one has got to . . . even from the moral point of view it is necessary, whatever one may say. Incidentally, I shall promptly smile, perhaps even laugh a little, then everyone will feel reassured. . . . I may joke once more with the bride, h'm. . . . I can even do this: I can hint that I'll return again exactly in nine months in the capacity of godfather. Ha-ha! She is sure to give birth by that time. After all, these people breed like rabbits. Well, they'll all break into laughter, the bride will blush; I shall kiss her forehead with genuine affection, I may even give her my blessing and . . . tomorrow in the office everyone will know of my exploit. Tomorrow I shall be stern once more, exacting, even obdurate, but at the same time they will all know who I really am. They will know my soul, they will know my innermost self: 'As a chief he is strict, but as a man—he is a perfect angel!' That is how I shall win them over; I shall catch them by some small action which you will never imagine. They are sure to be won over; I am their father, they my children. . . . Come now, Your Excellency Stepan Nikiforovitch, go thou and do likewise. . . .

"Do you realize, do you understand that Pseldonymov will tell his children about how the General himself feasted and even drank at his wedding? And these children will tell their children, and they in their turn their grandchildren, as their most treasured recollection, how the high dignitary, the statesman (I shall be all this by then) had done them the honour, and so on, and so on. I shall raise the spirits of the downtrodden. I shall restore him to himself. . . . To think that he gets ten roubles salary a month! . . . If I were to repeat this, or something of the kind, five or ten times, I should achieve universal popularity. My action will be imprinted upon all hearts, and the devil only knows what may be the outcome of all this, of all this popularity, I mean . . ."

It is in this or a similar manner that Ivan Ilyitch talked the question over with himself. (Well, my friends, what can a man not say to himself, especially when he is in a somewhat odd state?) It took perhaps one minute for all these arguments to flash through his mind, and undoubtedly he would have contented himself with these reveries, and imagining Stepan Nikiforovitch brought to shame, would have quietly set off for home and retired to bed. And that would have been a good thing, too. But the trouble was that that particular moment was no ordinary one. As if on purpose at that same moment the self-satisfied faces of Stepan Nikiforovitch and Semyon Ivanovitch formed in his imagination.

"We shan't live up to it," Stepan Nikiforovitch had repeated with an artful glance.

"Ha-ha-ha!" chimed in Semyon Ivanovitch with his nastiest smile.

"Just let's see, whether we shan't live up to it," said Ivan Ilyitch so resolutely that his face actually flushed. He walked off the wooden pavement and directed his steps firmly across the road towards the house of his subordinate, the registrar Pseldonymov.

He was being led astray by his evil star. Passing briskly through the open gate, he kicked away contemptuously the long-haired mongrel which had long lost its voice and which, more from a sense of duty than ferocity, threw itself at his feet with a hoarse bark. He went along the path raised above the ground leading to the little covered porch which jutted out into the courtyard and, climbing three very rickety wooden steps, found himself in a tiny passage. Although a tallow candle end or some sort of nightlight was burning somewhere in the corner, Ivan Ilyitch was not saved from stepping with his left foot, clad in a galosh, into a dish of brawn which had been put out to set. Ivan Ilyitch bent down and, glancing round with curiosity, saw that there were two other similar dishes with aspic, as well as two moulds evidently full of blancmange. The squashed brawn rather disconcerted him and for one fleeting moment he considered the idea of slipping away immediately. But he decided this would be unworthy of him. Maintaining that nobody had seen him and that he would surely not be suspected, he hastily wiped his galosh to eradicate all traces, felt for the padded door, opened it, and found himself in a very small hall. One half of the hall was literally choked with various coats, fur jackets, cloaks, hoods, scarves and galoshes. In the other half the musicians had spread out: two violins, a flute and a double-bass, four men in all who, doubtless, had been picked up off the streets. They sat at a small plain wooden table and by the light of one tallow candle were scraping away with all their might at the last figure of the quadrille. Through the open door to the adjoining room the dancers could be seen in a haze of dust, tobacco smoke and kitchen vapours. An atmosphere of frantic merriment enveloped the whole company. Bursts of laughter, shouts and piercing shrieks were heard from the ladies. The men stamped like a squadron of horse. The commands of the Master of Ceremonies could be heard above the uproar, his collar unbuttoned and coat-tails flying. "Gentlemen, forward, *chain de dames,* balance!" and so on. Ivan Ilyitch, in a state of some excitement, flung off his fur coat and his galoshes and, with his sable hat in his hand, entered the room. By now he had given up reasoning.

For the first instant no one noticed him; they were all busy finishing the dance. Ivan Ilyitch stood as if stunned and could not make out a thing in this hotchpotch of ladies' dresses, men with cigarettes between their lips, which flitted by ... one lady's pale-blue scarf floated by, catching his nose. She was followed by a medical student, his hair all dishevelled as if swept by a whirlwind, who rushing by him in frenzied rapture gave him a hard push. An officer of some regiment, who was as tall as a barge-pole, also flashed past him. Someone who flew past, stamping with the rest, cried out in an unnaturally shrill voice: 'Eh-eh-ekh Pseldonymushka!" Beneath Ivan Ilyitch's feet the floor felt sticky: they had evidently waxed it. There must have been about thirty guests in the room, which was quite sizeable.

However, in another minute the quadrille was over, and almost immediately everything happened exactly as Ivan Ilyitch had imagined as he stood dreaming on the wooden pavement. The guests and dancers had not time to regain their breath and wipe their faces when a murmur ran through the room, an extraordinary whisper. All eyes, all faces turned quickly in the direction of the guest who had just entered. Then followed a general shuffling back as everyone gently retreated. They tugged at the clothes of those who had not noticed the visitor to attract their attention; these now looked round and immediately fell back with the rest. Ivan Ilyitch still stood in the doorway without advancing, while between him and the guests the gap, strewn with countless sweet-papers, tickets and cigarette ends, widened. Suddenly a young man stepped timorously forward; he wore the uniform of a civil servant and had bristly, light-coloured hair and a hooked nose. He stepped forward all hunched up, and looked at the guest in exactly the same way as a dog looks at his master when summoned to receive a beating.

"How do you do, Pseldonymov? Recognize me?" said Ivan Ilyitch, and instantly felt that he had said it extremely awkwardly; he also felt that at that moment he was perhaps committing the most dreadful piece of stupidity.

"Your E-e-excellency!" muttered Pseldonymov.

"Well, now! I have dropped in quite by chance, my friend; dropped in on my way home, as you have probably guessed."

But Pseldonymov obviously had guessed nothing. He stood there, his eyes wide open, terribly perplexed.

"I suppose you won't turn me out . . . Glad or not glad, we have to welcome our guests . . ." continued Ivan Ilyitch, continuing to feel embarrassed to the point of weakness. He wanted to smile but no longer could; he felt that to tell his humorous story about Stepan Nikiforovitch and Trifon was becoming progressively less and less possible. Yet Pseldonymov, as if purposely, would not emerge from his stupor, and continued foolishly gazing at him. Ivan Ilyitch winced, he felt that it wanted only a moment more for the whole situation to become grotesque.

"Perhaps I have disturbed you . . . I'll be going!" he muttered, and a certain nerve began to twitch in the right corner of his mouth. But Pseldonymov had recovered.

"Your Excellency, for goodness' sake . . . an honour . . ." he mumbled, bowing hastily. "Do us the honour of being seated . . ." and recovering still more he pointed with both hands to the sofa, from which the table had been pushed back to make room for the dancing.

Ivan Ilyitch felt easier in his mind and sank down on the sofa; immediately someone rushed forward to move the table towards it. He cast a glance round and noticed that he alone was seated, while all the others, even the ladies, were standing. This was a bad omen. But the moment had not yet come to reassure and encourage them. The guests were still backing away and before him Pseldonymov alone stood, hunched up, still comprehending nothing and no flicker of a smile on his face. It was an unpleasant situation; in fact, our hero at that moment experienced so much anguish that this invasion à la Haroun al Raschid, in accordance with his principles of behaviour towards inferiors, might really have been regarded as a heroic deed.

But suddenly another small bowing figure appeared beside Pseldonymov. To his unspeakable pleasure, not to say relief, Ivan Ilyitch at once recognized the chief clerk of his department, Akim Petrovitch Zubikov. He was not, of course, acquainted with him personally, but knew of him as a capable official and a man of few words. He rose immediately and held out his hand, his whole hand, not merely two fingers. Akim Petrovitch received it in the palms of both his with the greatest reverence. The General had triumphed; the situation was saved.

And, in fact, Pseldonymov had now become, so to speak, not the second but the third person. He could now tell the story directly to the head clerk, in an hour of necessity driven to accept him as a friend, even as a crony. While all Pseldonymov could do was to merely remain silent, trembling with awe. Consequently, the rules of propriety were observed. But it was essential to tell the story; Ivan Ilyitch felt this; he saw that all the guests expected something, that all the members of the household, crowded in the two doorways, were almost scrambling over each other to get a look and hear him speak. However, it was aggravating that the chief clerk, out of sheer stupidity, still would not sit down.

"What about you?" said Ivan Ilyitch, awkwardly pointing to the place on the sofa by his side.

"If you please, sir . . . I am fine here, sir. . . ." And Akim Petrovitch quickly sat down on a chair which was swiftly offered to him by Pseldonymov, who still persisted in standing.

"Just imagine . . ." began Ivan Ilyitch, addressing Akim Petrovitch only, at first a little shakily but then in a voice tinged with familiarity. He even drawled slightly, stressing each word, emphasizing syllables, mispronouncing letters; in short, he was conscious of his affectation, but was no longer able to regain control of himself: some external force directed him. At that moment he was painfully becoming aware of a great many things.

"Just think, I have come straight from Stepan Nikiforovitch—you may perhaps have heard of him, the Privy Councillor—the one—you know . . . on that commission . . ."

Akim Petrovitch respectfully bent his whole body forward, conveying that he could hardly not know of him.

"He is now your neighbour," continued Ivan Ilyitch, for a moment turning to Pseldonymov in order to be correct and polished; but he soon looked away as he saw at once by Pseldonymov's eyes that he was quite indifferent to what he heard.

"The old man, as you know, has dreamed all his life of buying a house. . . . Well, he has bought one. A most attractive house. Yes . . . and it also happened to be his birthday. He has never celebrated it before. You know, he even used to conceal the date from us, ignored it out of meanness." He chuckled. "And now he is so delighted with his new house that he invited me and Semyon Ivanovitch. Do you know him—Shipulenko?"

Akim Petrovitch bowed again. He bowed eagerly. Ivan Ilyitch felt a little more relieved. Otherwise it had already occurred to him that the head clerk might perhaps guess that he was at that moment a necessary prop for His Excellency. That would be the worst that could happen.

"Well, the three of us sat down together; he treated us to champagne; we talked about business, one thing and another . . . about various subjects . . . we even had an argument . . . ha-ha!"

Akim Petrovitch raised his eyebrows respectfully.

"But that's not the point. At last I took my leave of him— he's an old man of regular habits, goes to bed early in his old age, you know. I left the house. My coachman, Trifon, was no- where to be seen. I got worried and made inquiries: 'What has Trifon done with my carriage?' It transpired that, in the hope that I should be late, he'd gone off to the wedding of his sister . . . God knows who, somewhere here on the Petersburg Side, and, as it happens, had taken the carriage with him!"

Once again, for courtesy's sake, the General glanced at Pseldonymov. The latter bowed immediately, but not at all in the way one would bow to a General. "He's unsympathetic and hard," flashed through Ivan Ilyitch's mind.

"You don't say!" said Akim Petrovitch in great astonish- ment, and a low murmur of surprise ran through the assem- bled company.

"You can imagine my position . . ." Ivan Ilyitch glanced round the room. "There was nothing left for me to do but to begin walking. I thought that if I reached the Bolshoi Prospect I should be sure to find some Vanka or other. Ha! ha! ha!"

"Ha! ha! ha!" echoed Akim Petrovich respectfully. Once more a murmur, this time of amusement, ran through the as- sembly. At that moment the glass of one of the lamps hanging on the wall splintered and broke. Someone rushed forward to deal with it. Pseldonymov gave a start and stared sternly at the lamp, but the General paid no attention whatsoever to it, and once again all was calm.

"There I was, walking along—the night was so lovely, so still. Suddenly I heard music, the stamping of feet, the sound of dancing. I inquired of the policeman what was going on. I was told it was Pseldonymov's wedding. Well, my friend, you *are* throwing a party on a grand scale, aren't you? Ha! ha!" he said suddenly, addressing Pseldonymov again.

"Ha! ha! ha! Yes, sir . . ." echoed Akim Petrovitch; the guests stirred, but the most absurd part of it was that, even now, though he bowed again, Pseldonymov still did not smile. He looked as though he was made of wood. "He must be a fool," thought Ivan Ilyitch. "Why, the old ass should smile and everything would go off smoothly." His heart throbbed with impatience.

"I'll drop in on my subordinate, I thought. After all, he won't kick me out . . . welcome or unwelcome, guests must be received. Forgive me, my friend, if I have inconvenienced you in any way. I shall leave. . . . I only dropped in for a moment."

But by this time the assembled company was gradually becoming restless. Akim Petrovitch assumed a sweet expression: "As if Your Excellency could possibly disturb us!" The guests stirred and at last began to show signs of being at their ease. Nearly all the ladies were now seated, which was a good and positive sign. The boldest of them were fanning themselves with their handkerchiefs. One lady, in a worn velvet dress, said something in a deliberately loud voice. The officer to whom she had addressed herself wanted to reply in a loud voice too, but as no one else was speaking loudly thought better of it

The men, mostly Government clerks with one or two students among them, exchanged glances, as if encouraging one another to relax, began coughing and actually moving a step or two in either direction. As a matter of fact, no one was particularly embarrassed; it was simply that they were awkward and regarded the man who had barged in on them and interrupted their merrymaking with something verging on hostility. The officer; ashamed of his feebleness, gradually began to sidle up to the table.

"Look, my friend, may I ask your name and patronymic?" Ivan Ilyitch inquired of Pseldonymov.

"Porfiry Petrov, Your Excellency," he answered, staring ahead as if he were on parade.

"Introduce me, Porfiry Petrov, to your young wife. . . . Take me to her. . . . I . . ."

And he made as if to rise. But Pseldonymov threw himself as fast as he could towards the drawing-room. As it happened, the bride was already standing at the door, but hearing her name mentioned she quickly hid herself. In a second Pseldonymov was leading her in by the hand. Everyone stepped aside, making way for them. Ivan Ilyitch rose solemnly and turned to her with his most amiable smile.

"I am very very pleased to meet you," he said with a slight bow, in the manner of a grand seigneur, "especially on such a day. . . ."

He gave a significant smile. The ladies became pleasantly agitated.

"*Charmée*," said the lady in the velvet dress, under her breath.

The bride was worthy of Pseldonymov. She was a slim young lady of barely seventeen, with a very tiny pale face, and sharp little nose. Her small, swivelling eyes did not in the least suggest shyness, but, on the contrary, stared fixedly and indeed a shade maliciously. Clearly Pseldonymov had chosen her for her beauty. She wore a white muslin dress over a pink slip. Her neck was scraggy, her body like that of a pullet, with protruding bones. She found simply nothing to say in reply to the General's greeting.

."That's a sugar plum, you have there," he continued in a low voice, as if addressing Pseldonymov alone, but purposely in such a way that the bride would hear him also. But again Pseldonymov had absolutely nothing to say, and this time he did not even make as if to bow. By his eyes it seemed to Ivan Ilyitch almost as though there were something cold and secret hidden within him, even something sly, peculiar and sinister. Yet at all costs he must provoke an emotional response from him. That, after all, was why he was here.

"Not a bad pair," he thought. "However . . ." and he turned again to the bride, who had seated herself on the sofa beside him. But he only got "no" or "yes" in answer to the one or two questions he addressed to her, and to tell the truth he could hardly even make these words out.

"If only she were slightly less embarrassed," he went on to reflect, "then I could start joking. As it is, I am in a hopeless fix." Akim Petrovitch also remained silent, as if on purpose; it was unpardonable, even though it was out of stupidity.

"Ladies and gentlemen, are you sure I have not interrupted your fun?" he was saying to the whole party. He even felt the palms of his hands sweating.

"No, sir . . . don't worry about that, Your Excellency, we shall begin again in a minute; just now . . . we are taking a breather, sir . . ." answered the officer. The bride gave the officer a look of appreciation; he was still young and wore the uniform of some obscure regiment. Pseldonymov had remained standing on the same spot, his head inclined slightly forward, his hooked nose seeming to jut out farther than ever. He listened, with the look of a footman holding his master's coat, waiting for the end of the letter's leave-taking. Ivan Ilyitch thought up this comparison himself; he felt bewildered and awkward, dreadfully awkward, as if the ground were giving way under his feet, as though he had entered some place of no return, as if he were in the dark.

All at once the guests made way for a short, stocky, middle-aged woman; she was dressed simply—though smartened up—with a large shawl round her shoulders, pinned at the throat, and a cap, which she was obviously unaccustomed to wearing. In her hands she held a small round tray on which stood an untouched, uncorked bottle of champagne and two glasses—no more and no less. The bottle was evidently intended for only two of the guests.

The elderly woman approached the General.

"Accept us for what we are, Your Excellency," she said, bowing, "and since you have deigned to honour my son's wedding with your presence, out of the goodness of your heart drink a toast to the young couple. Don't offend us by refusing."

Ivan Ilyitch clutched at her as if at salvation. She was by no means an old woman, not more than forty-five or -six. But she had such a kind, rosy face, an open, round Russian face—she smiled so good-naturedly, bowed so simply, that Ivan Ilyitch was almost comforted and was again filled with hope.

"So you, you are the . . . mother of your son," he said, rising from the sofa.

"My mother, Your Excellency," mumbled Pseldonymov, stretching his long neck and again thrusting his nose forward.

"Ah, very pleased . . . very pleased to meet you."

"Your Excellency won't refuse . . ."

"Not at all. I'd be delighted."

The tray was placed on the table. Pseldonymov jumped forward to pour out the wine, and, still standing, Ivan Ilyitch took a glass.

"I am particularly glad of this opportunity to be able—" he began—"to be able . . . to witness this . . . In short, as your chief, I wish you, madam," he turned to the bride, "and you, my friend Porfiry—I wish you all prosperity and lifelong happiness."

With feeling, he emptied his glass; it was the seventh that evening. Pseldonymov looked on seriously, even gloomily. The General began to detest him with all his might.

"And this blockhead here" (he glanced at the officer) "is still hanging around her. Couldn't he give a cheer? Then things would go like a house on fire. . . ."

"And you too, Akim Petrovitch, drink a glass and congratulate them," added the elderly woman, turning to the head clerk. "You are his chief, he is your subordinate. Look after my son's interests, my dear; I ask you as his mother. And don't forget us in times to come, love, Akim Petrovitch, kind man that you are."

"What excellent people these old Russian women are!" thought Ivan Ilyitch. "She has put new life into us all. I've always loved the common people. . . ."

Just then another tray was brought to the table. It was carried by a maidservant in a rustling new cotton dress and crinoline. The tray was so large that she could hardly hold it in her two hands. On it stood any number of small dishes with apples, bonbons, glacé fruits, jellied sweets, walnuts and many other things. Until then the tray had been standing in the drawing-room as refreshments for all the guests in particular for the ladies. But now it was brought in for the General alone.

"Don't refuse our refreshments, Your Excellency; what's ours is yours," said the elderly woman, bowing.

"Indeed, no, it's a pleasure," said Ivan Ilyitch; and he gladly took a walnut and cracked it between his fingers. After all, had he not decided to be as agreeable as possible.

Meanwhile, the bride burst into giggles.

"What's the joke?" asked Ivan Ilyitch, smiling, pleased to see any sign of animation.

"It is just Ivan Kostenkinytch who is making me laugh," she answered, lowering her eyes.

The General noticed a fair-haired, rather good-looking young man, hiding himself on a chair behind the sofa, whispering something to Mrs. Pseldonymov. The young man half rose; he was evidently very young and shy.

"I was telling her about the 'Book of Dreams', a book which interprets dreams, Your Excellency," he murmured almost apologetically.

"What sort of Book of Dreams?" asked Ivan Ilyitch indulgently.

"It's a new Book of Dreams, sir, quite a reputable one! I told her, sir, that if one dreamt of Mr. Panayev, that meant spilling coffee on one's shirt-front, sir."

"There's Innocence for you!" thought Ivan Ilyitch, with a feeling of irritation. Though the young man blushed as he spoke, he was nevertheless very pleased with himself for telling this story about Mr. Panayev.

"Yes, yes, I have heard of it," responded His Excellency.

"No, but there's an even better one," put in another voice quite close to Ivan Ilyitch. "A new encyclopaedia is being published, Mr. Krayevski is to write for it, they say, and Alferaki will be a contributor too . . . and there will be scurrilous pieces . . ."

This was said by a young man who, far from being timid, was rather bold in manner. He wore a white waistcoat and gloves and held a hat in his hands. He did not dance and, since he was on the staff of the satirical magazine *The Firebrand*, he behaved with an air of superiority that he lent to the company in which he found that he was by chance an honoured guest. He and Pseldonymov were on intimate terms with each other, having a year previously lived together in some obscure *quartier.* However, he did not say no to a glass of vodka and had already retired repeatedly for that purpose to a secluded back room which everyone was acquainted with. The General took a violent dislike to him.

"And what is so funny, sir," joyfully put in the fair-hatred young man who had told the story of the shirt-front, and whom the journalist in the white waistcoat consequently regarded with hate, "what is so funny, Your Excellency, is that the speaker assumed that Mr. Krayevski does not know how to spell and thinks that 'scurrilous' is written with an 'a'."

But the poor young man hardly had time to finish. He could see by the General's eyes that he had long been acquainted with this fact and that, as a result, he felt embarrassed. The young man felt abashed; he rapidly managed to make himself inconspicuous and remained dejected for the rest of the evening. However, the bold journalist on *The Firebrand* approached nearer, as though he intended to sit down somewhere in the vicinity of the General. This kind of familiarity seemed to Ivan Ilyitch a little presumptuous.

"Come, Porfiry, tell me—" began the General, for something to say, "I have always wanted to ask you personally—why are you called Pseldonymov and not Pseudonymov? Surely you ought to be called Pseudonymov?"

"I can give no precise reason, Your Excellency," answered Pseldonymov.

"Perhaps it was his father, sir, when he entered the service; there may have been some mistake in the papers, and he has remained Pseldonymov," suggested Akim Petrovitch. "It can happen."

"Un-doubt-ed-ly," took up the General eagerly, "un-doubt-ed-ly, you can judge for yourself—Pseudonymov has its origin in the literary word 'pseudonym', but Pseldonymov doesn't mean anything."

"Out of ignorance, sir," added Akim Petrovitch.

"How do you mean, out of ignorance?"

"Sometimes the common people change the letters out of ignorance, sir, and pronounce them in their own way. For example, they say 'nevalid' when they should say 'invalid', sir."

"Oh, yes, 'nevalid' . . . Ha! ha! ha! . . ."

"They also say 'mumber,' Your Excellency," blurted out the tall officer, who had long been itching to say something himself.

"What do you mean by 'mumber'?"

"'Mumber' instead of 'number', Your Excellency."

"Oh, yes, quite, 'mumber' instead of 'number' . . . Oh, yes, yes . . . ha! ha! ha!"

Ivan Ilyitch felt also obliged to give a little laugh for the officer's sake.

The officer adjusted his tie.

"And they also say 'bast'," broke in the contributor to *The Firebrand*. But His Excellency tried not to listen to him. After all, he was not obliged to laugh for everybody's sake.

" 'Bast' instead of 'past'," badgered the journalist with obvious annoyance.

Ivan Ilyitch looked at him severely.

"What are you bothering him for?" whispered Pseldonymov to the journalist.

"What do you mean? I am just making conversation. Can't a man even talk?" he was on the point of continuing the argument in a whisper, but instead he held his tongue and left the room with concealed anger.

He went straight to the back room, which had been made attractive to the gentlemen by a small table covered with a Yaroslav tablecloth on which were two sorts of vodka, herrings, small pieces of bread with caviar, and a bottle of extremely strong Russian sherry, which had been placed there for their benefit at the beginning of the evening. Still fuming, he had just finished pouring himself a glass of vodka when the medical student with the dishevelled hair suddenly rushed in. He was the chief dancer and can-can expert at Pseldonymov's ball. In hasty greed he attacked the decanter.

"They are going to begin directly," he muttered quickly in a dictatorial manner. "Come and have a look. I shall give them a solo performance standing on my head, and after supper I shall risk a can-can. It will be quite the thing for a wedding. A kind of friendly hint to Pseldonymov . . . she's a poppet that Cleopatra Semyonovna; you can risk anything you like with her."

"He's a reactionary," answered the journalist gloomily, emptying his glass.

"Who is a reactionary?"

"That individual who was treated to jellied sweets. He's a reactionary, I tell you."

"Go on with you," muttered the student, and hearing the *ritornella* of the quadrille, rushed out of the room.

Left alone, the journalist poured himself another glass to support his courage and independence, drained it and helped himself to the savouries; never has His Excellency State Councillor Ivan Ilyitch had a more bitter enemy or a more implacable avenger than the slighted contributor to *The Firebrand*, especially after two glasses of vodka. Alas! Ivan Ilyitch was totally unsuspecting. Furthermore, he was oblivious of another very important fact, which was to affect the attitude of the guests towards His Excellency. The fact was that though he, for his part, had given a proper and even detailed explanation of his presence at the wedding of a subordinate, this explanation had not really satisfied anybody and the guests continued to feel ill at ease. But suddenly, as if by magic, everything changed; they seemed reassured and ready to enjoy themselves, laugh, scream and dance, just as if the unexpected guest were not present in the room. The reason for this was that suddenly, by some mysterious means, a whispered rumour spread the news that the guest seemed "just a little bit . . . too merry on account of . . ." And although on the surface this rumour seemed dreadful slander, it became more and more evident that it was true and explained everything. The company relaxed. And it was at that very moment that the quadrille, the last before supper to which the medical student had hurried back, began.

Ivan Ilyitch was just on the point of addressing the bride again, trying this time to overcome her shyness with a joke, when the tall officer ran up and with a flourish sank down on one knee before her. She immediately jumped up from the sofa and flitted off with him to take her place in the quadrille. The officer did not even apologize, nor did she glance at the General on leaving him; it seemed as if she were glad to be rid of him.

"After all, she really was justified in doing that," thought Ivan Ilyitch; "they haven't learnt good manners. H'm! You, my friend, Porfiry, don't stand on ceremony," he said, addressing Pseldonymov. "You may have business to attend to . . . some arrangements . . . or something. . . . Please don't mind me . . ."

"Is he standing guard over me, or something?" he added to himself.

He found Pseldonymov unbearable, with his long neck and his stare fixed in his direction. In short, all this was not as it should be, not at all as it should be, but Ivan Ilyitch was still far from admitting this to himself.

The quadrille began.

"May I, Your Excellency . . . ?" asked Akim Petrovitch respectfully, holding the bottle in his hands, poised to fill His Excellency's glass.

"I . . . I really don't know whether . . ."

But Akim Petrovitch, his face beaming with reverence, had already poured out the champagne. Filling one glass, he poured another for himself, furtively, stealthily, awkwardly grimacing, with one difference, that his own glass was about a finger's breadth less full, which seemed somehow more respectful. Seated beside his immediate superior, he felt like a woman in labour. What, in fact, was he to talk about? He felt in duty bound to entertain His Excellency, since he had the honour of his company. The champagne provided a way out of the situation, and besides, His Excellency welcomed the champagne—not for its own sake, for it was warm and quite horrible, but for the mere fact that it was being offered to him.

"The old fellow wants a drink himself," thought Ivan Ilyitch, "and doesn't dare to drink without me. I don't want to prevent him. And it would be odd for the bottle to stand neglected between us."

He took a gulp—at least it looked better than just sitting there like that.

"I am here, you see," he began, pausing and emphasizing each word, "you might say I just happen to be present, and, of course, some people might think it . . . so to speak . . . improper . . . for me to be present at such a gathering. . . ."

Akim Petrovitch remained silent and listened attentively with timid curiosity.

"But I hope you will understand why I am here. . . . After all, it's not just to drink wine that I've come, is it? . . . Ha! ha! ha!"

Akim Petrovitch wanted to laugh like His Excellency, but somehow broke off and once more failed to make a comforting response.

"I am here . . . as you might say, to sanction . . . to demonstrate, that is to say—the moral, that is to say, aim . . ." continued Ivan Ilyitch, getting annoyed with Akim Petrovitch for being so slow on the uptake; suddenly he fell silent too. He noticed that poor Akim Petrovitch was actually lowering his eyes in guilt. The General hastened, in some confusion, to take another gulp from his glass, while Akim Petrovitch, as if his whole salvation depended on it, seized the bottle and refilled the glass. "You certainly are dumb," thought Ivan Ilyitch, looking sternly at poor Akim Petrovitch. The latter, sensing the General's glance upon him, finally decided to remain silent and not to raise his eyes. Thus they remained seated opposite each other for about two minutes—two rather painful minutes for Akim Petrovitch.

Just one or two words about Akim Petrovitch. Timid as a rabbit, he was of the old school, brought up to accept subservience while at the same time being a kind and worthy man. He was a native of Petersburg, that is to say, his father and grandfather were born and bred in Petersburg and had worked there and never once been out of the town. Men like Akim Petrovitch belong to quite a peculiar class of Russian people. They know nothing about Russia, which really doesn't worry them. All their interests are centred in Petersburg, and particularly, in their place of employment. All their attention is directed to games of chance at kopeck points, to their place of work and their monthly salary. They do not know a single Russian custom nor a single Russian song except *Lutchinushka*, and this only thanks to the barrel organs. Incidentally, there exist two infallible signs by which one can immediately tell a true Russian from a Petersburg Russian: the first is that Petersburg Russians, without exception, never say "*The Petersburg Journal*", but always "*The Academic Journal*". The second and equally important sign is that they never say "breakfast", but always "Frühstück", with a special emphasis on the "Früh". By these well-established and distinctive signs one can recognize them anywhere. In brief, they represent a submissive type which has definitely emerged during the last thirty years. But Akim Petrovitch was no fool. Had the General asked him something within his sphere, he would have made an appropriate answer and kept up the con-

over to his *vis-à-vis*, managed quickly to press a few dozen kisses to it. His lady floated before him, appearing quite oblivious to what was going on. The medical student actually did dance a solo on his head and provoked frenzied raptures, stamps of approval and screams of delight. In a word, the lack of inhibition was remarkable.

Ivan Ilyitch, who was also under the influence of the wine, at first began by smiling, but little by little a kind of bitter doubt began to seep into his soul: of course he very much approved of the easy manners and freedom; it is this that he has wanted, even in his heart willing this freedom when they had all hung back, but already it was getting out of control. For example, the lady in the well-worn blue velvet dress which looked as though it had been bought not second- but fourth-hand, had pinned it up so high during the sixth figure of the quadrille that it looked as if she wore trousers. This was that same Cleopatra Semyonovna, with whom one could risk anything, according to the expression used by her partner, the medical student. As for the medical student, no words could describe him: he was a wizard, a regular Fokine. How had it all happened? At one time they were diffident, and now they were rapidly becoming free and easy. Unimportant as this transition seemed, it was somehow strange and threatening; just as if they had completely forgotten the existence of Ivan Ilyitch. Naturally, he was the first to burst out laughing and even risked clapping. Akim Petrovitch politely giggled in chorus with him, with obvious pleasure and no suspicion that His Excellency was already beginning to nurture yet another viper in his bosom.

"You dance famously, young man," Ivan Ilyitch felt obliged to say to the student, who passed by at the end of the quadrille.

The student turned sharply to him, made some sort of grimace and rudely drawing up his face close to His Excellency's crowed like a cock at the top of his voice. This was altogether too much. Ivan Ilyitch rose from the table. In spite of this, a volley of uncontrollable laughter burst out, for the cock-crow sounded amazingly real, and the grimace was quite unexpected. Ivan Ilyitch was still standing perplexed, when suddenly Pseldonymov himself appeared and, bowing, invited him to supper. His mother followed.

"Your Excellency, sir," she said, bowing, "do us the honour—don't scorn our poverty . . ."

"I . . . I—really don't know . . ." began Ivan Ilyitch. "I did not come for this. . . . I was just thinking of going."

In fact, he was already holding his fur hat in his hands. Moreover, at this very instant, he promised himself he would go immediately, at all costs, and not stay for anything—but . . . he stayed.

A minute later he led the procession to the supper table. Pseldonymov and his mother walked before him, clearing the way. They seated him in the place of honour and again an unopened bottle of champagne appeared before him. To begin with there was herring and vodka. He stretched out his hand, filled himself a huge wineglass of vodka and drained it. He never had before touched vodka. He felt as if he were rolling downhill, flying, flying so that he must hold on, cling to something, but this was no longer possible.

Really, his position was becoming more and more of an anomaly. Moreover, it seemed as though Fate was mocking at him.

God knows what had happened to him in less than an hour. On entering he had, so to speak, stretched out his arms to embrace the whole of mankind and all his subordinates; and here scarcely an hour had gone by and he was painfully realizing only too clearly that he hated Pseldonymov and cursed him, his wife and his wedding. As if that were not enough, he could see from Pseldonymov's face, by his eyes alone, that the latter hated him too; he was staring at him almost saying: "Damn you. What the hell have you tagged on to me for?" He had long ago read all this in Pseldonymov's eyes.

Of course, even now, Ivan Ilyitch, as he sat down at table, would sooner have had his hand cut off than admit frankly, even to himself let alone out loud, that all this was in fact so. That moment had not yet come; he still retained some moral equilibrium, though something was steadily gnawing at his heart. He felt his heart crying out for freedom, space to breathe and quietude. After all, Ivan Ilyitch was too good a man, really!

Did he not know full well that he ought to have left long ago; not merely left, but more, saved himself; that all this had suddenly turned out very different from what he had expected, from the way he had imagined things when he was walking along the raised wooden pavement earlier.

What did I come here for? Did I come here to eat and drink? he asked himself as he helped himself to some herrings. He even felt certain misgivings. He felt a momentary sense of irony at his own actions; he began to ask himself why he had entered. But how could he leave? Simply to leave without seeing it through was impossible. What will people say? They'll say I frequent the wrong places. Indeed, that's what it'll look like if I don't see things through to the end. What will they say tomorrow, for instance (since the news is sure to spread)? What will Stepan Nikiforovitch and Semyon Ivanovitch say, what will they say at the office, at Shembel's, at Shubin's? No, I must leave in such a way that they will all understand why I came; I must reveal my moral aim. . . . Yet that sublime moment declined to present itself. "They don't even respect me," he continued. "What are they laughing about? They are so free and easy, as if they lack any kind of feeling. . . . Yes, I have long suspected the whole younger generation of lacking sensitivity. I must stay, at all costs! . . . They have been dancing, but now at table they will all be gathered together. . . . I shall talk about current affairs, reforms, the greatness of Russia . . . I may yet succeed in interesting them. Yes! Perhaps nothing is yet lost. . . . Perhaps this is how it always happens in real life. If only I knew how to set about winning them over. What sort of approach shall I make? I feel completely lost. . . . And what do they want, what are they asking for? I can see they are sniggering over there. Good Lord, surely not about me! But what is it I want? Why am I here, why don't I go away, what do I hope to accomplish? . . . He thought all this, and a kind of shame, a kind of deep, unbearable shame, rent his heart.

From then on, events took their own course.

Two minutes after he had sat down at table, he was struck by a terrible realization. He suddenly felt horribly drunk, not as he had been before, but totally, absolutely drunk. The cause of it was the glass of vodka which he had drained immediately after the champagne and which had taken effect at once. He felt, sensed with his whole being, that he was completely helpless.

Of course, he appeared to be far more confident, but his consciousness did not forsake him and cried out: "It is wrong, very wrong, and also utterly revolting." Of course, the rambling, drunken thoughts could not concentrate on any one point; at once, almost tangibly, two opposing selves appeared within him. In the one self was confidence, the desire to gain a victory, surmount all obstacles, and the desperate conviction that he could reach his goal. The other made itself felt by anguish, by a kind of bleeding of the heart. "What will they say? How will all this end? What will happen tomorrow—Tomorrow . . . ?"

Earlier in the evening he had had a vague feeling that he had enemies among the guests. "That was because I was drunk when I came in," he thought, in agonizing doubt. To his increasing horror he now became convinced, through unmistakable signs, that some of those at table really were his enemies and that this could no longer be doubted.

"And why? What is it all for?" he mused.

At this table all the guests were seated, thirty of them; among them some had finally passed out. The others conducted themselves with a somewhat negligent, flaunting independence, shouting at the tops of their voices, prematurely proposing toasts, shooting bread pellets at the ladies. One very ill-favoured individual in a dirty frock-coat fell off his chair as soon as he had seated himself at table and remained on the floor right to the end of the supper. Another was determined to climb on the table to propose a toast, and it was only the officer who restrained his ill-timed enthusiasm by seizing him by his coat-tails. The supper was quite commonplace, although a chef had been engaged, the serf of some general or other. There was brawn, tongue with potatoes, meat rissoles with green peas, and finally, blancmange for dessert. There was beer, vodka and sherry to drink. The bottle of champagne stood before the General alone, which obliged him to help himself and also Akim Petrovitch, who at supper did not dare to act on his own initiative. The other guests were meant to drink the toasts in bitters, or whatever they could get hold of. The table itself was made up of a number of smaller ones and included even a card table. They were covered with several tablecloths, among them a coloured Yaroslav one. Men and women were seated alternately at table. Pseldonymov's mother would not sit down; she bustled about and attended to the guests. And now a spiteful-looking female appeared who had not been there before; she wore a russet silk dress and the highest possible cap and had her face bandaged up as though she had toothache. This was the bride's mother, who had finally consented to come in to supper from the back room. Until then she had not left her room because of her irreconcilable hostility towards Pseldonymov's mother; but of this we shall speak later. The lady gave a malicious, almost scornful look at the General and evidently did not want to be introduced to him. Ivan Ilyitch was highly suspicious of her. But others were suspect besides, and instilled unwitting apprehension and uneasiness. It seemed almost as though they were involved in some conspiracy together directed against Ivan Ilyitch. At least, that is how it seemed to him, and as supper progressed he became more and more convinced of this. For example, there was an evil-looking gentleman with a small beard, some kind of self-styled artist; he actually looked several times at Ivan Ilyitch and then turned to whisper in the ear of his neighbour. Another, a student, admittedly completely drunk, judging by certain signs, was nevertheless suspect. There was little hope for the medical student either; even the officer was not entirely to be relied on. But it was the journalist from *The Firebrand* who was generating a peculiar and obvious hatred: he had a manner of lounging in his chair, with an extremely proud and arrogant air, sniffing with such self-assurance. And though the other guests paid no attention to the journalist (who had merely written four lines of verse for *The Firebrand*, which made him a liberal) and evidently positively disliked him, still when a small bread pellet suddenly fell beside Ivan Ilyitch, obviously intended for him, he was ready to swear that the culprit was none other than the contributor to *The Firebrand*.

Naturally, all this affected him for the worse.

He made yet another particularly unpleasant observation. Ivan Ilyitch was quite convinced that he was beginning to pronounce his words with difficulty and indistinctly; he wanted to say a great deal, but his tongue would not move; also his memory would suddenly have lapses and, worse still, he would suddenly burst out laughing for no reason at all. This condition soon passed after Ivan Ilyitch had helped himself to a glass of champagne without wanting it particularly, but suddenly gulping it down without further thought. As a result, he almost burst into tears. He felt he was succumbing to a most peculiar sentimentality. He began to love everyone again, even Pseldonymov, even the contributor to *The Firebrand*. He suddenly wanted to embrace them all, to forget everything and make peace with them. More, he wanted quite freely to tell them everything, everything, everything; that is, what a good and admirable fellow he was, what splendid abilities he possessed, what service he would be to his country, how well he could amuse the ladies, and, above all, how progressive he was, in what an idealistic manner he was prepared to condescend to all, even to the very lowest; and finally, to conclude, he would frankly describe all the motives that had induced him, an uninvited guest, to turn up at Pseldonymov's, drink two bottles of his champagne and give him the pleasure of his company.

"The truth above all, sacred truth and frankness; I'll win them with frankness. They will believe me, I can see it so clearly; they look at me with positive hostility, but when I reveal everything I'll win them over, there's no doubt of it. They will fill up their glasses and drink my health. The officer, I am sure, will break his glass on his spur. They may even shout 'Hurrah!' Even if they should decide to toss me up in the Hussar manner, I would not resist that either; it might even be a good thing. I shall kiss the bride on the forehead; she is a sweet thing. Akim Petrovitch also is a very nice man. Pseldonymov, of course, will improve in time. He lacks the polish of the *beau monde*. . . . And though the whole of this new generation lacks that certain sensitivity, yet I shall tell them about Russia's standing among the Great Powers. I will also mention the peasant question, yes, and . . . they will all love me and I'll emerge crowned in glory. . . ."

These fantasies, naturally, were very pleasant; the only unpleasant thing amidst all these rosy hopes was that Ivan Ilyitch suddenly discovered in himself one more unexpected talent, that is, for spitting. At any rate, spittle began suddenly to spurt from his lips, quite involuntarily. He noticed it first of all on Akim Petrovitch, whose cheek he had bespattered and who, out of respect, sat there without daring to wipe it off. Ivan Ilyitch took a napkin and suddenly wiped it off himself. Yet at once this action seemed to him so absurd, so remote from all reason, that he fell silent and began to wonder. Akim Petrovitch, though he had had some drink, sat there just as if he had been scalded. Ivan Ilyitch now realized that he had been talking to him for almost a quarter of an hour on a most interesting subject, but Akim Petrovitch, as he listened to him, appeared not only embarrassed but even afraid of something. Also Pseldonymov, who was sitting one chair away from him, craned his long neck, and with his head on one side, seemed to be listening with a most unpleasant expression in his face. It was as if he was keeping an eye on him. . . . Glancing around at the guests he noticed that many were looking straight at him and roaring with laughter. But strangest of all, this did not embarrass him in the least; on the contrary, he sipped at his glass once more and began to talk so that everyone could hear.

"As I have just said to Akim Petrovitch," he began as loudly as possible, "ladies and gentlemen, Russia . . . particularly Russia . . . in one word, you understand what I want to s-say . . . . Russia is experiencing, it is my deepest conviction, a mood of idealism . . ."

"Idealism!" echoed from the other end of the table.

"Hu-hu!"

"Tu-tu!"

Ivan Ilyitch was cut short. Pseldonymov rose from his chair and began to look round. Who was it who was shouting? Akim Petrovitch surreptitiously shook his head, as if reproving the guests. Ivan Ilyitch saw this clearly, but suffered in silence.

"Idealism," he continued stubbornly—"not long ago . . . just so . . . not long ago I said to Stepan Nikiforovitch . . . yes . . . that—that the rebirth, so to speak, of things . . ."

"Your Excellency!" somebody cried out from the other end of the table.

"Sir?" answered Ivan Ilyitch, interrupted, trying to make out who was addressing him.

"Nothing at all, Your Excellency, I got carried away. Continue! Co-on-tin-ue!" the same voice was heard again.

Ivan Ilyitch winced.

"The rebirth, so to speak, of these very things . . ."

"Your Excellency," shouted the same voice.

"What do you want?"

"How do you do!"

This time Ivan Ilyitch could stand it no longer. He broke off his speech and turned to the offender. He was still quite a young student, completely drunk, who looked exceedingly suspect. For a long time he had been shouting, and even broken a glass and two plates, asserting that this was the done thing at weddings. At the moment when Ivan Ilyitch turned to him, the officer had set about dealing severely with the rowdy.

"What's wrong; what are you yelling for? You should be sent out, that would be best."

"It's not about you, Your Excellency, not about you. Carry on!" cried the tipsy student, sprawling in his chair. "Carry on, I am listening and I am very pleased by you. It is praiseworthy, most praiseworthy."

"A drunken schoolboy!" Pseldonymov suggested in a whisper.

"I see he is drunk, but . . ."

"I have just told a funny story, Your Excellency," began the officer, "about a lieutenant of our regiment who talked to his superiors in just the same way; and the young man here is imitating him. He added to every word his superior said his own

'Praiseworthy' . . . For this he got discharged from the service ten years ago."

"What—what-t lieutenant was it?"

"One in our regiment, Your Excellency. He was mad about praising. At first he was cautioned, then later he was put under arrest. . . . His chief reproved him in a fatherly manner; but he only said 'praiseworthy'. It was strange, a fine sort of fellow he was—over six foot tall. They thought of having him tried, but then realized that he was insane."

"So he's a schoolboy. Well, one need not be too strict about schoolboy tricks. For my part, I am ready to forgive . . ."

"There was a medical examination, Your Excellency."

"How? Did they dissect him?"

"Good gracious, no; he was quite alive, sir."

A loud and almost universal burst of laughter came from the guests, who had at first tried to behave in a respectable manner. Ivan Ilyitch was embarrassed.

"Gentlemen, gentlemen," he cried, for the first time with hardly a stutter; "I am quite capable of grasping that one cannot dissect a living man. . . . I assumed that owing to his being insane he was no longer alive . . . that is to say, he was dead. . . . I mean to say . . . that you do not love me . . . whereas I love all of you; yes, I love Por . . . Porfiry. . . . I am lowering myself by speaking like this. . . ."

At that moment a huge gob of spittle flew out of Ivan Ilyitch's mouth and landed on the tablecloth with a splash, on a most conspicuous spot. Pseldonymov rushed to wipe it off with a napkin. This last misfortune finally crushed him.

"Gentlemen, this is just too much!" he cried out in despair.

"The man is tight, Your Excellency," Porfiry was on the point of putting in.

"Porfiry! I see that you . . . all . . . yes! I am saying that I hope . . . yes, I invite you all to say in what way I have lowered myself?" Ivan Ilyitch was on the verge of tears.

"Your Excellency, for goodness' sake, sir!"

"Porfiry, I appeal to you . . . Tell me, if I came . . . yes, yes, to the wedding, I had a purpose. I set out to raise your moral standards. . . . I wanted you to feel . . . I am appealing to you all: have I lowered myself very much in your eyes or have I not?"

Silence persisted. That was just it—dead silence, and after such a direct question, too! "Well, what would it cost them to say something at least?" flashed through His Excellency's mind. But the guests merely exhanged glances. Akim Petrovitch sat there more dead than alive, while Pseldonymov, struck dumb with fear, repeated the terrible question that had long before presented itself to him, under his breath: "And what will be the consequence of all this tomorrow?"

All of a sudden the contributor to *The Firebrand*, now completely drunk, who until then had been sitting in sullen silence, turned to Ivan Ilyitch and with flashing eyes began to answer on behalf of the whole company:

"Yes, sir!" he shouted in a thundering voice, "yes, sir, you have lowered yourself, yes, you are a reactionary . . . re-actionary!"

"Young man, come to your senses! Who d'you think you're talking to?" cried Ivan Ilyitch furiously, jumping up again from his chair.

"You; and furthermore, I am not 'young man' . . . you have come here to show off and to play for popularity."

"Pseldonymov, what is this?" cried out Ivan Ilyitch.

However, Pseldonymov had jumped up in such terror that he was rooted to the ground and was completely at a loss. The guests seated at the table had been struck dumb too. The artist and the student were applauding and shouting "Hear, hear!"

The journalist continued to shout with unrestrained fury:

"Yes, you came here to boast of your ideals. You have disrupted everyone's enjoyment. You have been drinking champagne and never considered that it was too expensive for a Government clerk on a salary of ten roubles a month. And I suspect that you are one of those chiefs who have a taste for the young wives of their employees. Not only that, but I am thoroughly convinced that you uphold the payment of compensation. . . . Yes, yes, yes!"

"Pseldonymov! Pseldonymov!" cried Ivan Ilyitch, stretching his arms towards him. He felt that each word of the journalist was a fresh dagger in his heart.

"At once, Your Excellency, please, don't worry," Pseldonymov cried hysterically, running up to the journalist, seizing him by the collar and dragging him away from the table. No one would have expected such a display of physical strength from the feeble Pseldonymov. But the journalist was very drunk, while Pseldonymov was completely sober. He punched him several times in the back and pushed him out of the door.

"You are all scoundrels," shouted the journalist. "I'll show you up in *The Firebrand* tomorrow. . . ."

Everyone rose.

"Your Excellency, Your Excellency," cried Pseldonymov, his mother and several of the guests, crowding round the General, "Your Excellency, calm yourself."

"No, no," cried the General, "I am destroyed. . . . I came . . . I wanted, so to speak, to give my blessing. . . . And this, for this . . ."

He sank on to a chair as if he were fainting, put both hands on the table and dropped his head on to them, straight into a plate of blancmange. No need to describe the general horror. After a minute he got up, evidently wanting to go away, staggered, tripped over the leg of a chair, fell on the floor with full force and began to snore. . . .

This kind of thing happens to people not accustomed to drink when by chance they do get drunk. Down to the last detail, up to the last moment they retain consciousness and then suddenly they black out completely. Ivan Ilyitch lay unconscious on the floor. Pseldonymov seized himself by the hair and stood rooted to the ground. The guests were breaking up hurriedly, each commenting on the occurrence in his own way. It was already nearly three o'clock in the morning.

What complicated matters was that to Pseldonymov the affair was far worse than one could imagine, taking into account even the unpleasantness of the present situation. While Ivan Ilyitch is lying on the floor with Pseldonymov standing beside him tearing his hair in despair, let us digress to put in a few words of explanation about Porfiry Petrovitch Pseldonymov himself.

It was not more than a month before his wedding that he was on the verge of total and irrevocable disaster. He came from the provinces, where his father had held some post or other and had died while he was awaiting trial for some offence. When, five months before his wedding, Pseldonymov, who in Petersburg had been facing disaster for a whole year, obtained his appointment at ten roubles salary, he felt restored in body and soul, but he was soon humbled once again by circumstances. Of the Pseldonymov family there remained only two people in the whole world, himself and his mother, who had left her native place in the provinces after her husband's death. Mother and son lived in cold and hunger. There were days when Pseldonymov himself went with a mug to the Fontanka to get a drink of water. Having obtained a job, he and his mother managed to settle somewhere in a tenement. She set about washing linen for other people, while in four months he scraped together enough money to acquire a pair of boots and an old coat. And what misery he had to undergo in his office: his superiors would come up to him, asking when he had last had a bath. Rumour had it that whole nests of bugs had settled under the collar of his uniform. But Pseldonymov had a strong character. In appearance he was gentle and quiet; his education had been very sketchy, he was hardly ever heard to talk. I simply don't know whether he ever thought, ever made plans, evolved systems, ever indulged in day-dreaming at all. But instead of this he had developed an instinctive, determined unconscious resolve to work his way out of his unfortunate circumstances. He was as tenacious as an ant; if you destroy an ants' nest, they start building it again; destroy it a second time and they will start once more, and so on, without respite. He was an orderly and domesticated creature. It was written all over his face that he would make his way, build his nest and perhaps even put something by for a rainy day. His mother was the only person in the whole wide world who loved him, and she loved him passionately. She was strong, indefatigable, a hard-working woman, and at the same time, kind. They would have continued to live in their tenement for five or six years perhaps, until things had changed, had they not come across the retired Titular Councillor Mlekopitayev. The latter was a former treasurer in a Government office of their native district, who had since established himself and settled with his family in Petersburg. He knew Pseldonymov, and had been in some way indebted to his father. He had not much money put by, of course, but he had some; how much, in fact, nobody knew, neither his wife, his eldest daughter, nor his relations. He had two daughters, and as he was pig-headed, a drunkard, a petty tyrant and, to crown it all, an invalid, he suddenly took it into his head to marry off one of his daughters to Pseldonymov. "I know him," he said, "his father was a good man, and the son will be a good man too." Whatever Mlekopitayev wanted to do, he did; and once he said a thing was to happen, it did happen. He was a singularly pig-headed man. He spent most of the time sitting in an arm-chair, as he had lost the use of his legs through some kind of illness, which, however, did not prevent him from drinking vodka. He spent whole days drinking and abusing people. He was a vicious man, and sure to be tormenting someone all the time. For this purpose be kept several distant relatives in the house; his sister, a sick and cantankerous woman, two of his wife's sisters, both bad-tempered and with long tongues; as well as his old aunt, who had managed to break a rib. Besides them, he kept another sponger, a Russified German woman, because of her talent for telling stories out of the *Arabian Nights*. His only pleasure was to nag these unfortunate hangers-on, to swear at them every minute, like a trooper, though none of them, not even his wife, who had been born with a chronic toothache, ever dared utter a word. He caused them to quarrel among themselves, invented and provoked gossip and dissensions, and then broke out into laughter, delighted to see them on the verge of coming to blows. He was very glad when his eldest daughter, who had lived in poverty for ten years with her officer husband, finally, when she was widowed, came to live in his house with her three small, sickly children. He could not bear her children, but because the number of victims on whom he could make his daily experiments increased with their arrival, the old man was very pleased. This whole crew of spiteful women and sick children were squeezed, together with their torturer, into a wooden house on the Petersburg Side. They never had enough food, because the old man was miserly and only gave money by kopecks, though he never grudged it for his vodka; they never had enough sleep because the old man suffered from insomnia and demanded to be amused. In short—all of them lived in misery and cursed their fate. It was at that time that Mlekopitayev noticed Pseldonymov. He was impressed by his long nose and his submissive manner. His sickly, plain youngest daughter was then just seventeen. Though she had been to a German school at one time, she had never learned much more than the alphabet. After that she continued to grow up, consumptive and anaemic, under the blows of her crippled and drunken father, in a turmoil of domestic gossip, spying and slander. She had no friends, and she was devoid of common sense. For a long time she had longed to get married. In the company of strangers she was silent but at home with her mother and the spongers she was spiteful, and sharp as a gimlet. She particularly liked to slap and pinch her sister's children, telling on them for taking sugar and bread, which caused eternal and ceaseless rows between her and her honour. Pseldonymov knew very well that his bride loathed him and would far rather have married an officer. But he bore it all, in accordance with the arrangements he and his mother had made. Throughout the day of the wedding, and the whole evening, the old man swore horribly as he sat drinking. Because of the wedding, the whole family had taken refuge in the back rooms and were so crowded together they were almost suffocating. The front rooms were intended for dancing and supper. At last, when, at eleven o'clock, the old man fell asleep, dead drunk, the bride's mother, who had been snarling at Pseldonymov's mother on that day more than ever, decided to change her tune and turn up at the party. The appearance of Ivan Ilyitch had upset everything. Mrs. Mlekopitayev was disconcerted; she was offended and began to scold them for not having warned her beforehand that the General himself was invited. She was assured that he had come of his own accord, uninvited, but she was so stupid that she would not believe this.

When champagne was required, all Pseldonymov's mother could find was just one rouble. Pseldonymov himself had not a kopeck. They were compelled to humble themselves before the angry Mrs. Mlekopitayev and beg money first for one bottle of champagne, then for another. They pointed out future business connections, the career to come, they did their utmost to persuade her. At last she consented to part with her money, but in return she nagged at Pseldonymov with such bitterness that he kept running into the chamber and throwing himself on the bridal couch, intended for heavenly delights, silently tearing his hair and trembling all over with impotent rage. Ivan Ilyitch had no idea of the price of the two bottles of champagne he had drunk that evening. How great was the terror of Pseldonymov, his anguish and even despair, when the business of Ivan Ilyitch took such an unexpected turn: he could anticipate the worries, the piercing shrieks and tears from the capricious bride, which would perhaps continue throughout the whole night, with reproaches from the bride's stupid relations. As it was, his head was already aching and he felt dazed. And here was Ivan Ilyitch requiring assistance; at three o'clock in the morning a doctor had to be found and a carriage to take him home; it had to be a carriage, since it would be impossible to dispatch such a personage, in such a state, to his home in a simple cab or sledge. But where was he to find the money even so much as for a carriage?

Mrs. Mlekopitayev, enraged that the General had not spoken two words to her and had not even looked at her during the whole of supper, declared that she had not a kopeck. Perhaps she really had not got a kopeck to her name. But where was he to get the money? What was he to do? Yes, he had good reason to tear his hair.

Meanwhile, Ivan Ilyitch was carried to a little leather sofa that stood there ready in the dining-room. While the tables were cleared and sorted out, Pseldonymov rushed hither and thither to raise some money; he even tried to borrow from the servants, but he found that nobody had any. He dared to trouble Akim Petrovitch, who had stayed longer than the others. But kind as he was, at the sound of the word "money" he became so bewildered and indeed frightened that he talked a lot of surprising nonsense: "At any other time, I would with pleasure . . ." he mumbled, "but now . . . really you must excuse me . . ." And picking up his hat, he quickly fled from the house.

Only the kind-hearted young man who had told the story about the Book of Dreams gave some help, but even this was pulled out from beneath someone —but where to put it? The upshot was that the bed must be made up in the drawing-room, the point farthest away from the bulk of the family and with its own exit. But what was the bed to be made up on? Simply on chairs? Everyone knows that only boys who are home from school for the weekend are made to sleep on chairs; for someone of Ivan Ilyitch's standing this would be most disrespectful. What would he say tomorrow at finding himself lying on a couple of chairs? Pseldonymov would not even hear of it. There was only one thing left to do: to carry him to the bridal couch. This bridal couch, as we have already said, had been set up in a little room leading from the dining-room. On the double bed was a newly bought, as yet unused mattress, clean bed linen, four pillows, in pink-coloured calico slips, under flounced muslin covers. The eiderdown was of pink satin, quilted in patterns. From a gilt ring above the bed fell muslin curtains. In a word, everything was as it should be, and the guests, who had nearly all visited the bed-room, had admired the fineries. The bride, though she could not bear Pseldonymov, had several times during the evening come into the room, quite secretly, to have a good look. Imagine her indignation, her fury, when she heard that they wanted to put the sick man, who was ill with cholera or something, on her bridal couch. The bride's mother began to take her part, cursed, and vowed she would complain the next day to her husband, but Pseldonymov held his own and insisted: Ivan Ilyitch was transferred to the double bed, and a bed was made up on chairs for the young couple in the drawing-room. The bride snivelled and wanted to pinch someone, but she dared not disobey; she knew well that Papa had a stick and that next day he would be sure to require a detailed report of what occurred.

cry—it was a cry of the most sinister kind. Immediately following it a noise could be heard, a crash as if chairs were falling, and all at once a whole crowd of screaming and frightened women at every stage of undress rushed into the still, darkened room. These women were the bride's mother, her elder sister, who had abandoned her sick children for the time being, and three of her aunts—even the one with the broken rib had dragged herself along. The cook was there too; even the sponger, the German woman with the talent for telling stories, had come along. It was the latter's feather bed, the best in the house and her own and sole property, that had been forcibly removed from under her for the use of the young couple. All these shrewd respectable women had already, a quarter of an hour earlier, been stealing on tiptoe from the kitchen, through the corridor, and had been eavesdropping in the hall, consumed by the most inexplicable curiosity. Meanwhile, somebody hastily lit a candle and an unexpected sight was revealed. The chairs, unable to withstand the weight of two people and the broad feather bed which they supported on either side, had given way and the mattress had fallen between them to the floor. The bride was trembling with rage; this time she was wounded to her very heart. Pseldonymov, morally crushed, stood there like a criminal caught in the act. He did not even try to justify himself. Exclamations and shrieks were heard on all sides; hearing the noise, Pseldonymov's mother also came running up, but this time the bride's mother got the upper hand entirely. First she blamed Pseldonymov, for the most part unjustly saying: "What sort of a husband are you, my dear sir, in view of this? What use are you, my dear sir, after this disgrace?" and so on, and, finally, taking her daughter by the hand, led her away from her husband to her own room, taking it upon herself to account for this tomorrow when her fierce husband would demand an explanation. All the others departed with her, sighing and shaking their heads. His mother alone stayed with Pseldonymov and tried to comfort him. But he immediately drove her away.

He was in no condition to be comforted. He reached the sofa and sat down in a spirit of gloomy reflection; there he sat, barefooted, dressed only in his underwear. His mind was confused. Now and again he glanced in a mechanical fashion round the room where only recently there had been such wild dancing and where cigarette smoke still hung in the air. Cigarette-ends and sweet-papers were still scattered on the stained and dirty floor. The wreck of the bridal bed and the overturned chairs bore witness to the transitory nature of the best and truest earthly hopes and dreams. He remained like this for almost an hour. Depressing thoughts came into his head: what awaited him at the office? He realized that at all costs he would have to change his place of work; it would be impossible to stay on where he was after what had happened last night. Into his mind, too, came Mlekopitayev, who would probably on the morrow force him to dance the Kazatchek once more to test his docility. He realized that although Mlekopitayev had given fifty roubles towards the wedding expenses—which had all been spent to the last kopeck—he had not thought to let them have the four hundred roubles promised as dowry, nor even made further mention of them. Even the house had not been officially transferred to his name. His thoughts also turned to his wife, who had left him at the most critical moment of his life; he thought of the tall officer who had gone down on one knee before her.

This he had already contrived to notice; he thought of the seven devils which possessed his wife, according to the personal testimony of her father, and of the stick ready to drive them out. . . . Of course, he felt he was capable of enduring much, but Fate had in the outcome allowed such surprises to assail him that it was finally understandable that he should doubt his own strength. Thus Pseldonymov grieved. Meanwhile the candle-end was burning low. Its flickering light, falling straight on to Pseldonymov's profile, reflected it on the wall in a huge image, with outstretched neck, a hooked nose and two tufts of hair sticking up over his forehead and at the back of his head. At last, when the first breath of morning freshness came, he got up, shivering and his feelings numbed, reached the feather bed which was lying between the chairs, and, without putting anything right, without blowing out the candle-end, without even slipping a pillow under his head, he crawled into the bed, overcome by that leaden, death-like sleep which is experienced perhaps by those who are condemned to public execution on the morrow.

On the other hand, what could compare with the agonizing night which Ivan Ilyitch Pralinski spent on the bridal couch of the unfortunate Pseldonymov? For a long time headache, vomiting and other most unpleasant attacks gave him not a moment's peace. This was infernal torment. His occasional flashes of awareness lit up such an abyss of terror, such grim and horrible images, that it would have been better for him to have remained unconscious. However, everything was still confused in his head. For instance, he recognized Pseldonymov's mother—he heard her gentle remonstrances: "Try to bear it, my pet, try to bear it, dearie, it'll be all right, you'll see." He recognized her but could not logically account for her presence. Horrible visions came to him: most often he saw Semyon Ivanovitch; but looking more closely he observed that it was not Semyon Ivanovitch at all, but Pseldonymov's nose. Before him flitted by the self-styled artist and the officer, the old woman with her face bound up. He was preoccupied most of all with the gilt ring hanging above his head, from which hung the muslin curtains. He made it out quite clearly in the dim light of the candle-end which illuminated the room, and all the time he was pondering; what was it made for? He asked the elderly woman about it several times, but evidently he said something other than what he intended, for she seemed not to understand him, however much he tried to explain. At last, as morning came near, the attacks ceased and he fell into a sound, dreamless sleep. He slept for the best part of an hour and when he awoke he was almost fully conscious; he felt he had an unbearable headache and the nastiest possible taste in his mouth and on his tongue which appeared to be made of woollen cloth. He raised himself on the bed, looked round, and reflected. The pale light of the breaking day penetrated through the chinks of the shutters in a narrow line, trembling on the wall. It was almost seven o'clock in the morning. But when Ivan Ilyitch suddenly realized and remembered all that had happened to him from the beginning of the previous evening; when he remembered all the mishaps at supper, his exploit that misfired, his speech at table; when suddenly, with terrifying vividness, the possible consequences of all this presented themselves to him, what people would now think and say about him; when he looked round and, finally, saw to what a sad and disordered state he had reduced the peaceful bridal couch of his subordinate—oh, then, such deadly shame, such torment filled his heart that he cried out, covered his face with his hands and, in despair, threw himself on to the pillow. A minute later he jumped out of bed and saw that his clothes were lying on the chair, neatly folded and already cleaned; he seized them and quickly began to struggle into them, looking around as if in dreadful fear of something. Here too, on the other chair, lay his fur coat, his fur hat with his yellow gloves. He was on the point of slipping quietly away. But suddenly the door opened and Pseldonymov's mother entered, carrying an earthenware basin and a jug. Over her shoulder hung a towel. She put the basin down and without further argument declared that he most certainly needed a wash.

"Come, come! My dear sir, you must wash, you can't go without washing. . . ."

In that instant Ivan Ilyitch realized that if there were a single person in the whole world before whom he need not be ashamed and whom he need not fear, it was this same elderly woman. He did wash. And long afterwards, in painful moments of his life, he remembered, along with other regrettable occasions, all the circumstances of this awakening: this earthenware basin and china jug filled with cold water in which bits of ice were still floating, the oval cake of soap with some kind of embossed lettering on it, wrapped in pink paper, which must have cost fifteen kopecks, bought evidently for the newly-weds and used by Ivan Ilyitch; and he remembered the elderly woman with the linen towel over her left shoulder. The cold water refreshed him; he rubbed himself dry and, without saying a word, without even thanking his nurse, he seized his fur hat, threw his fur coat, which Pseldonymov's mother handed to him, over his shoulder, and ran through the corridor, through the kitchen, where the cat was already mewing and the cook raising herself from her bed to look at him with avid curiosity, out into the street and flung himself into a passing cab. The morning was frosty, a chilly yellowish mist still blanketed the houses and everything else. Ivan Ilyitch turned up his collar. He felt that everybody was looking at him, that everybody knew him, that everybody would know . . .

For eight days he did not leave the house, nor did he appear at the office. He was ill, painfully ill, but more in his mind than his body. In those eight days he endured complete purgatory and, surely, they would be credited to him in the next world. There were moments when he thought of taking monastic vows. Truly, he had such moments; his imagination even began to play actively along those lines. He dreamed of quiet singing in cloisters, an open coffin, life in a solitary cell, woods and caves; but as soon as he came to himself he confessed that it was all terrible nonsense and exaggeration, and was ashamed of it. Then came pangs of mental anguish about his wasted life. Then shame once more filled his heart, overwhelmed it in an instant, and turned a knife in the wound. He shuddered as he recalled certain images. What would they say about him, what would they think about him when he entered the office, what whisperings would pursue him for a whole year, for ten years, for his whole life? The story of this disgraceful affair would be told to future generations. Sometimes he became so faint-hearted that he was ready to drive at once to Semyon Ivanovitch and ask him for forgiveness and for his friendship. He did not even try to justify himself, he blamed himself completely: he could find no excuse for himself and was ashamed of his inability to do so.

He also contemplated resigning his post immediately and dedicating himself, without fuss, in solitude, to the happiness of mankind. In any case, it was undoubtedly necessary to relinquish all his acquaintances and even to go so far as to eradicate all memory of himself. But then it occurred to him that this, too, was nonsense, and that with increased strictness towards his subordinates the whole thing could still be put right. This gave him hope and courage. Finally, after eight whole days of doubt and torment, he felt that he could no longer bear the uncertainty, and one fine morning he decided to set off for the office.

Previously, while he was still sitting at home in distress, he had pictured to himself a thousand times how he would enter his office. He was completely convinced that he was sure to hear ambiguous whisperings, that he would see suspicious faces, reap most malicious smiles. Imagine his surprise when, in fact, nothing of the kind happened. He was received respectfully; everyone bowed to him; all were serious; all were busy. When he reached his private room, joy filled his heart.

He at once and most conscientiously took up his work, listened to several reports and explanations, issued decisions. He felt that never till now had he reasoned and made decisions so well, with such judgment, so competently, as on that morning. He saw that they were pleased with him, respected him, esteemed him. The most sensitive susceptibility would have felt nothing. Everything went off splendidly.

At last Akim Petrovitch himself appeared with some papers. At sight of him Ivan Ilyitch felt as if something had struck him right to the heart, but only for a moment. He gave him his attention, talked in a measured manner, showed how things should be done and cleared up certain points. He noticed only that he avoided glancing for long at Akim Petrovitch, or, rather, that Akim Petrovitch was afraid to look at him. But then Akim Petrovitch had finished, and began to collect his papers.

"There is just one request," he began, as impassively as possible. "Official Pseldonymov asks to be transferred to the Department of——. His Excellency Semyon Ivanovitch Shipulenko has promised him a position. Pseldonymov asks for your kind co-operation, Your Excellency."

"I see, he wishes to be transferred," said Ivan Ilyitch, feeling that a great weight had been taken off his mind. He glanced at Akim Petrovitch, and in that instant their eyes met

"Well now, I, for my part . . . I will use . . ." replied Ivan Ilyitch, "I am prepared . . ."

It was plain to see that Akim Petrovitch wanted to slip away as quickly as possible. But suddenly Ivan Ilyitch, in a burst of magnanimity, decided to get the thing off his chest once and for all. He had evidently had another inspiration.

"Tell him," he began, directing a piercing and meaningful glance towards Akim Petrovitch. "Convey to Pseldonymov that I bear him no ill will. . . . Yes, I bear none. . . . That, on the contrary, I am quite prepared to forget the past, to forget everything, everything. . . ."

But suddenly, Ivan Ilyitch stopped short, amazed at the strange behaviour of Akim Petrovitch, when, for no reason whatever, he changed all of a sudden from a sensible person into a most awful fool. Instead of listening, and letting Ivan Ilyitch finish, he blushed very foolishly, bowing rather hurriedly and awkwardly, bobbing, at the same time receding towards the door. His whole appearance revealed the desire to sink through the floor, or, rather, to reach his desk as quickly as possible. Ivan Ilyitch, left alone, rose from his chair in confusion. He looked into the mirror and did not see his own face.

"No! discipline, discipline and again discipline," he whispered almost unconsciously, and suddenly his face burned. He felt more shame, more heaviness at heart, than he had experienced during even the most unbearable moments of his eight days of illness.

"I have failed to live up to my ideals!" he said to himself, and sank into his chair—helpless.

THE DREAM OF A RIDICULOUS MAN

A Fantastic Story

TRANSLATED BY DAVID MAGARSHACK

ing. I've always cut a ridiculous figure. I suppose I must have known it from the day I was born. At any rate, I've known for certain that I was ridiculous ever since I was seven years old. Afterwards I went to school, then to the university, and—well—the more I learned, the more conscious did I become of the fact that I was ridiculous. So that for me my years of hard work at the university seem in the end to have existed for the sole purpose of demonstrating and proving to me, the more deeply engrossed I became in my studies, that I was an utterly absurd person. And as during my studies, so all my life. Every year the same consciousness that I was ridiculous in every way strengthened and intensified in my mind. They always laughed at me. But not one of them knew or suspected that if there were one man on earth who knew better than anyone else that he was ridiculous, that man was I. And this—I mean, the fact that they did not know it—was the bitterest pill for me to swallow. But there I was myself at fault. I was always so proud that I never wanted to confess it to anyone. No, I wouldn't do that for anything in the world. As the years passed, this pride increased in me so that I do believe that if ever I had by chance confessed it to any one I should have blown my brains out the same evening. Oh, how I suffered in the days of my youth from the thought that I might not myself resist the impulse to confess it to my schoolfellows. But ever since I became a man I grew for some unknown reason a little more composed in my mind, though I was more and more conscious of that awful characteristic of mine. Yes, most decidedly for some unknown reason, for to this day I have not been able to find out why that was so. Perhaps it was because I was becoming terribly disheartened owing to one circumstance which was beyond my power to control, namely, the conviction which was gaining upon me that nothing in the whole world *made any difference*. I had long felt it dawning upon me, but I was fully convinced of it only last year, and that, too, all of a sudden, as it were. I suddenly felt that it made *no* difference to me whether the world existed or whether nothing existed anywhere at all. I began to be acutely conscious that *nothing existed in my own lifetime*. At first I couldn't help feeling that at any rate in the past many things had existed; but later on I came to the conclusion that there had not been anything even in the past, but that for some reason it had merely seemed to have been. Little by little I became convinced that there would be nothing in the future, either. It was then that I suddenly ceased to be angry with people and almost stopped noticing them. This indeed disclosed itself in the smallest trifles. For instance, I would knock against people while walking in the street. And not because I was lost in thought—I had nothing to think about—I had stopped thinking about anything at that time: it made no difference to me. Not that I had found an answer to all the questions. Oh, I had not settled a single question, and there were thousands of them! But *it made no difference to me*, and all the questions disappeared.

And, well, it was only after that that I learnt the truth. I learnt the truth last November, on the third of November, to be precise, and every moment since then has been imprinted indelibly on my mind. It happened on a dismal evening, as dismal an evening as could be imagined. I was returning home at about eleven o'clock and I remember thinking all the time that there could not be a more dismal evening. Even the weather was foul. It had been pouring all day, and the rain too was the coldest and most dismal rain that ever was, a sort of menacing rain—I remember that—a rain with a distinct animosity towards people. But about eleven o'clock it had stopped suddenly, and a horrible dampness descended upon everything, and it became much damper and colder than when it had been raining. And a sort of steam was rising from everything, from every cobble in the street, and from every side-street if you peered closely into it from the street as far as the eye could reach. I could not help feeling that if the gaslight had been extinguished everywhere, everything would have seemed much more cheerful, and that the gaslight oppressed the heart so much just because it shed a light upon it all. I had had scarcely any dinner that day. I had been spending the whole evening with an engineer who had two more friends visiting him. I never opened my mouth, and I expect I must have got on their nerves. They were discussing some highly controversial subject, and suddenly got very excited over it. But it really did not make any difference to them. I could see that. I knew that their excitement was not genuine. So I suddenly blurted it out. "My dear fellows," I said, "you don't really care a damn about it, do you?" They were not in the least offended, but they all burst out laughing at me. That was because I had said it without meaning to rebuke them, but simply because it made no difference to me. Well, they realised that it made no difference to me, and they felt happy.

When I was thinking about the gaslight in the streets, I looked up at the sky. The sky was awfully dark, but I could clearly distinguish the torn wisps of cloud and between them fathomless dark patches. All of a sudden I became aware of a little star in one of those patches and I began looking at it intently. That was because the little star gave me an idea: I made up my mind to kill myself that night. I had made up my mind to kill myself already two months before and, poor as I am, I bought myself an excellent revolver and loaded it the same day. But two months had elapsed and it was still lying in the drawer. I was so utterly indifferent to everything that I was anxious to wait for the moment when I would not be so indifferent and then kill myself. Why—I don't know. And so every night during these two months I thought of shooting myself as I was going home. I was only waiting for the right moment. And now the little star gave me an idea, and I made up my mind then and there that it should *most certainly* be that night. But why the little star gave me the idea—I don't know.

And just as I was looking at the sky, this little girl suddenly grasped me by the elbow. The street was already deserted and there was scarcely a soul to be seen. In the distance a cabman was fast asleep on his box. The girl was about eight years old. She had a kerchief on her head, and she wore only an old, shabby little dress. She was soaked to the skin, but what stuck in my memory was her little torn wet boots. I still remember them. They caught my eye especially. She suddenly began tugging at my elbow and calling me. She was not crying, but saying something in a loud, jerky sort of voice, something that did not make sense, for she was trembling all over and her teeth were chattering from cold. She seemed to be terrified of something and she was crying desperately, "Mummy! Mummy!" I turned round to look at her, but did not utter a word and went on walking. But she ran after me and kept tugging at my clothes, and there was a sound in her voice which in very frightened children signifies despair. I know an army officer, on a visit to Petersburg with her three little children who had all been taken ill since their arrival at our house. She and her children were simply terrified of the captain and they lay shivering and crossing themselves all night long, and the youngest child had a sort of nervous attack from fright. This captain (I know that for a fact) sometimes stops people on Nevsky Avenue and asks them for a few coppers, telling them he is very poor. He can't get a job in the Civil Service, but the strange thing is (and that's why I am telling you this) that the captain had never once during the month he had been living with us made me feel in the least irritated. From the very first, of course, I would not have anything to do with him, and he himself was bored with me the very first time we met. But however big a noise they raised behind their partition and however many of them there were in the captain's room, it makes no difference to me. I sit up all night and, I assure you, I don't hear them at all—so completely do I forget about them. You see, I stay awake all night till daybreak, and that has been going on for a whole year now. I sit up all night in the armchair at the table—doing nothing. I read books only in the daytime. At night I sit like that without even thinking about anything in particular: some thoughts wander in and out of my mind, and I let them come and go as they please. In the night the candle burns out completely.

I sat down at the table, took the gun out of the drawer, and put it down in front of me. I remember asking myself as I put it down, "Is it to be then?" and I replied with complete certainty, "It is!" That is to say, I was going to shoot myself. I knew I should shoot myself that night for certain. What I did not know was how much longer I should go on sitting at the table till I shot myself. And I should of course have shot myself, had it not been for the little girl.

II

You see, though nothing made any difference to me, I could feel pain, for instance, couldn't I? If anyone had struck me, I should have felt pain. The same was true so far as my moral perceptions were concerned. If anything happened to arouse my pity, I should have felt pity, just as I used to do at the time when things did make a difference to me. So I had felt pity that night: I should most decidedly have helped a child. Why then did I not help the little girl? Because of a thought that had occurred to me at the time: when she was pulling at me and calling me, a question suddenly arose in my mind and I could not settle it. It was an idle question, but it made me angry. What made me angry was the conclusion I drew from the reflection that if I had really decided to do away with myself that night, everything in the world should have been more indifferent to me than ever. Why then should I have suddenly felt that I was not indifferent and be sorry for the little girl? I remember that I was very sorry for her, so much so that I felt a strange pang which was quite incomprehensible in my position. I'm afraid I am unable better to convey that fleeting sensation of mine, but it persisted with me at home when I was sitting at the table, and I was very much irritated. I had not been so irritated for a long time past. One train of thought followed another. It was clear to me that so long as I was still a human being and not a meaningless cipher, and till I became a cipher, I was alive, and consequently able to suffer, be angry, and feel shame at my actions. Very well. But if, on the other hand, I were going to kill myself in, say, two hours, what did that little girl matter to me and what did I care for shame or anything else in the world? I was going to turn into a cipher, into an absolute cipher. And surely the realisation that I should soon cease to exist *altogether*, and hence everything would cease to exist, ought to have had some slight effect on my feeling of pity for the little girl or on my feeling of shame after so mean an action. Why after all did I stamp and shout so fiercely at the little girl? I did it because I thought that not only did I feel no pity, but that it wouldn't matter now if I were guilty of the most inhuman baseness, since in another two hours everything would become extinct. Do you believe me when I tell you that that was the only reason why I shouted like that? I am almost convinced of it now. It seemed clear to me that life and the world in some way or other depended on me now. It might almost be said that the world seemed to be created for me alone. If I were to shoot myself, the world would cease to exist—for me at any rate. To say nothing of the possibility that nothing would in fact exist for anyone after me and the whole world would dissolve as soon as my consciousness became extinct, would disappear in a twinkling like a phantom, like some integral part of my consciousness, and vanish without leaving a trace behind, for all this world and all these people exist perhaps only in my consciousness.

I remember that as I sat and meditated, I began to examine all these questions which thronged in my mind one after another from quite a different angle, and thought of something quite new. For instance, the strange notion occurred to me that if I had lived before on the moon or on Mars and had committed there the most shameful and dishonourable action that can be imagined, and had been so disgraced and dishonoured there as can be imagined and experienced only occasionally in a dream, a nightmare, and if, finding myself afterwards on earth, I had retained the memory of what I had done on the other planet, and moreover knew that I should never in any circumstances go back there—if that were to have happened, should I or should I not have felt, as I looked from the earth upon the moon, that *it made no difference* to me? Should I or should I not have felt ashamed of that action? The questions were idle and useless, for the gun was already lying before me and there was not a shadow of doubt in my mind that *it* was going to take place for certain, but they excited and maddened me. It seemed to me that I could not die now without having settled something first. The little girl, in fact, had saved me, for by these questions I put off my own execution.

Meanwhile things had grown more quiet in the captain's room: they had finished their card game and were getting ready to turn in for the night, and now were only grumbling and swearing at each other in a halfhearted sort of way. It was at that moment that I suddenly fell asleep in my armchair at the table, a thing that had never happened to me before.

I fell asleep without being aware of it at all. Dreams, as we all know, are very curious things: certain incidents in them are presented with quite uncanny vividness, each detail executed with the finishing touch of a jeweller, while others you leap across as though entirely unaware of, for instance, space and time. Dreams seem to be induced not by reason but by desire, not by the head but by the heart, and yet what clever tricks my reason has sometimes played on me in dreams! And furthermore what incomprehensible things happen to it in a dream. My brother, for instance, died five years ago. I sometimes dream about him: he takes a keen interest in my affairs, we are both very interested, and yet I know very well all through my dream that my brother is dead and buried. How is it that I am not surprised that, though dead, he is here beside me, doing his best to help me? Why does my reason accept all this without the slightest hesitation? But enough. Let me tell you about my dream. Yes, I dreamed that dream that night. My dream of the third of November. They are making fun of me now by saying that it was only a dream. But what does it matter whether it was a dream or not, so long as that dream revealed the Truth to me? For once you have recognised the truth and seen it, you know it is the one and only truth and that there can be no other, whether you are asleep or awake. But never mind. Let it be a dream, but remember that I had intended to cut short by suicide the life that means so much to us, and that my dream—my dream—oh, it revealed to me a new, grand, regenerated, strong life!

Listen.

III

I have said that I fell asleep imperceptibly and even while I seemed to be revolving the same thoughts again in my mind. Suddenly I dreamed that I picked up the gun and, sitting in my armchair, pointed it straight at my heart—at my heart, and not at my head. For I had firmly resolved to shoot my-self through the head, through the right temple, to be precise. Having aimed the gun at my breast I paused for a second or two, and suddenly my candle, the table and the wall began moving and swaying before me. I fired quickly.

In a dream you sometimes fall from a great height, or you are being murdered or beaten, but you never feel any pain un-less you really manage somehow or other to hurt yourself in bed, when you feel pain and almost always wake up from it. So it was in my dream: I did not feel any pain, but it seemed as though with my shot everything within me was shaken and everything was suddenly extinguished, and a terrible dark-ness descended all around me. I seemed to have become blind and dumb. I was lying on something hard, stretched out full length on my back. I saw nothing and could not make the slightest movement. All round me people were walking and shouting. The captain was yelling in his deep bass voice, the landlady was screaming and—suddenly another hiatus, and I was being carried in a closed coffin. I could feel the coffin sway-ing and I was thinking about it, and for the first time the idea flashed through my mind that I was dead, dead as a doornail, that I knew it, that there was not the least doubt about it, that I could neither see nor move, and yet I could feel and reason. But I was soon reconciled to that and, as usually happens in dreams, I accepted the facts without questioning them.

And now I was buried in the earth. They all went away, and I was left alone, entirely alone. I did not move. Whenever before I imagined how I should be buried in a grave, there was only one sensation I actually associated with the grave, namely, that of damp and cold. And so it was now. I felt that I was very cold, especially in the tips of my toes, but I felt nothing else.

I lay in my grave and, strange to say, I did not expect anything, accepting the idea that a dead man had nothing to expect as an incontestable fact. But it was damp. I don't know how long a time passed, whether an hour, or several days, or many days. But suddenly a drop of water, which had seeped through the lid of the coffin, fell on my closed left eye. It was followed by another drop a minute later, then after another minute by another drop, and so on. One drop every minute. All at once deep indignation blazed up in my heart, and I suddenly felt a twinge of physical pain in it. "That's my wound," I thought. "It's the shot I fired. There's a bullet there. . . ." And drop after drop still kept falling every minute on my closed eyelid. And suddenly I called (not with my voice, for I was motionless, but with the whole of my being) upon Him who was responsible for all that was happening to me:

"Whoever Thou art, and if anything more rational exists than what is happening here, let it, I pray Thee, come to pass here too. But if Thou art revenging Thyself for my senseless act of self-destruction by the infamy and absurdity of life after death, then know that no torture that may be inflicted upon me can ever equal the contempt which I shall go on feeling in silence, though my martyrdom last for aeons upon aeons!"

I made this appeal and was silent. The dead silence went on for almost a minute, and one more drop fell on my closed eyelid, but I knew, I knew and believed infinitely and unshakably that everything would without a doubt change immediately. And then my grave was opened. I don't know, that is, whether it was opened or dug open, but I was seized by some dark and unknown being and we found ourselves in space. I suddenly regained my sight. It was a pitch-black night. Never, never had there been such darkness! We were flying through space at a terrific speed and we had already left the earth behind us. I did not question the being who was carrying me. I was proud and waited. I was telling myself that I was not afraid, and I was filled with admiration at the thought that I was not afraid. I cannot remember how long we were flying, nor can I give you an idea of the time; it all happened as it always does happen in dreams when you leap over space and time and the laws of nature and reason, and only pause at the points which are especially dear to your heart. All I remember is that I suddenly beheld a little star in the darkness.

"Is that Sirius?" I asked, feeling suddenly unable to restrain myself, for I had made up my mind not to ask any questions.

"No," answered the being who was carrying me, "that is the same star you saw between the clouds when you were coming home."

I knew that its face bore some resemblance to a human face. It is a strange fact but I did not like that being, and I even felt an intense aversion for it. I had expected complete non-existence and that was why I had shot myself through the heart. And yet there I was in the hands of a being, not human of course, but which *was*, which existed. "So there is life beyond the grave!" I thought with the curious irrelevance of a dream, but at heart I remained essentially unchanged. "If I must *be* again," I thought, "and live again at someone's unalterable behest, I won't be defeated and humiliated!"

"You know I'm afraid of you and that's why you despise me," I said suddenly to my companion, unable to refrain from the humiliating remark with its implied admission, and feeling my own humiliation in my heart like the sharp prick of a needle.

He did not answer me, but I suddenly felt that I was not despised, that no one was laughing at me, that no one was even pitying me, and that our journey had a purpose, an unknown and mysterious purpose that concerned only me. Fear was steadily growing in my heart. Something was communicated to me from my silent companion—mutely but agonisingly—and it seemed to permeate my whole being. We were speeding through dark and unknown regions of space. I had long since lost sight of the constellations familiar to me. I knew that there were stars in the heavenly spaces whose light took thousands of millions of years to reach the earth. Possibly we were already flying through those spaces. I expected something in the terrible anguish that wrung my heart. And suddenly a strangely familiar and incredibly nostalgic feeling shook me to the very core: I suddenly caught sight of our sun! I knew that it could not possibly be *our* sun that gave birth to our earth, and that we were millions of miles away from our sun, but for some unknown reason I recognised with every fibre of my being that it was precisely the same sun as ours, its exact copy and twin. A sweet, nostalgic feeling filled my heart with rapture: the old familiar power of the same light which had given me life stirred an echo in my heart and revived it, and I felt the same life stirring within me for the first time since I had been in the grave.

"But if it is the sun, if it's exactly the same sun as ours," I cried, "then where is the earth?"

And my companion pointed to a little star twinkling in the darkness with an emerald light. We were making straight for it.

"But are such repetitions possible in the universe? Can that be nature's law? And if that is an earth there, is it the same earth as ours? Just the same poor, unhappy, but dear, dear earth, and beloved for ever and ever? Arousing like our earth the same poignant love for herself even in the most ungrateful of her children?" I kept crying, deeply moved by an uncontrollable, rapturous love for the dear old earth I had left behind.

The face of the poor little girl I had treated so badly flashed through my mind.

"You shall see it all," answered my companion, and a strange sadness sounded in his voice.

But we were rapidly approaching the planet. It was growing before my eyes. I could already distinguish the ocean, the outlines of Europe, and suddenly a strange feeling of some great and sacred jealousy blazed up in my heart.

"How is such a repetition possible and why? I love, I can only love the earth I've left behind, stained with my blood when, ungrateful wretch that I am, I extinguished my life by shooting myself through the heart. But never, never have I ceased to love that earth, and even on the night I parted from it I loved it perhaps more poignantly than ever. Is there suffering on this new earth? On our earth we can truly love only with suffering and through suffering! We know not how to love otherwise. We know no other love. I want suffering in order to love. I want and thirst this very minute to kiss, with tears streaming down my cheeks, the one and only earth I have left behind. I don't want, I won't accept life on any other! . . ."

But my companion had already left me. Suddenly, and without as it were being aware of it myself, I stood on this other earth in the bright light of a sunny day, fair and beautiful as paradise. I believe I was standing on one of the islands which on our earth form the Greek archipelago, or somewhere on the coast of the mainland close to this archipelago. Oh, everything was just as it is with us, except that everything seemed to be bathed in the radiance of some public festival and of some great and holy triumph attained at last. The gentle emerald sea softly lapped the shore and kissed it with manifest, visible, almost conscious love. Tall, beautiful trees stood in all the glory of their green luxuriant foliage, and their innumerable leaves (I am sure of that) welcomed me with their soft, tender rustle, and seemed to utter sweet words of love. The lush grass blazed with bright and fragrant flowers. Birds were flying in flocks through the air and, without being afraid of me, alighted on my shoulders and hands and joyfully beat against me with their sweet fluttering wings. And at last I saw and came to know the people of this blessed earth. They came to me themselves. They surrounded me. They kissed me. Children of the sun, children of their sun—oh, how beautiful they were! Never on our earth had I beheld such beauty in man. Only perhaps in our children during the very first years of their life could one have found a remote, though faint, reflection of this beauty. The eyes of these happy people shone with a bright lustre. Their faces were radiant with understanding and a serenity of mind that had reached its greatest fulfilment. Those faces were joyous; in the words and voices of these people there was a child-like gladness. Oh, at the first glance at their faces I at once understood all, all! It was an earth unstained by the Fall, inhabited by people who had not sinned and who lived in the same paradise as that in which, according to the legends of mankind, our first parents lived before they rive from our science; for our science seeks to explain what life is and strives to understand it in order to teach others how to live, while they knew how to live without science. I understood that, but I couldn't understand their knowledge. They pointed out their trees to me, and I could not understand the intense love with which they looked on them; it was as though they were talking with beings like themselves. And, you know, I don't think I am exaggerating in saying that they talked with them! Yes, they had discovered their language, and I am sure the trees understood them. They looked upon all nature like that—the animals which lived peaceably with them and did not attack them, but loved them, conquered by their love for them. They pointed out the stars to me and talked to me about them in a way that I could not understand, but I am certain that in some curious way they communed with the stars in the heavens, not only in thought, but in some actual, living way. Oh, these people were not concerned whether I understood them or not; they loved me without it. But I too knew that they would never be able to understand me, and for that reason I hardly ever spoke to them about our earth. I merely kissed the earth on which they lived in their presence, and worshipped them without any words. And they saw that and let me worship them without being ashamed that I was worshipping them, for they themselves loved much. They did not suffer for me when, weeping, I sometimes kissed their feet, for in their hearts they were joyfully aware of the strong affection with which they would return my love. At times I asked myself in amazement how they had managed never to offend a person like me and not once arouse in a person like me a feeling of jealousy and envy. Many times I asked myself how about life eternal, but apparently they were so convinced of it in their minds that for them it was no question at all. They had no places of worship, but they had a certain awareness of a constant, uninterrupted, and living union with the Universe at large. They had no specific religions, but instead they had a certain knowledge that when their earthly joy had reached the limits imposed upon it by nature, they—both the living and the dead—would reach a state of still closer communion with the Universe at large. They looked forward to that moment with joy, but without haste and without pining for it, as though already possessing it in the vague stirrings of their hearts, which they communicated to each other.

In the evening, before going to sleep, they were fond of gathering together and singing in melodious and harmonious choirs. In their songs they expressed all the sensations the parting day had given them. They praised it and bade it farewell. They praised nature, the earth, the sea, and the woods. They were also fond of composing songs about one another, and they praised each other like children. Their songs were very simple, but they sprang straight from the heart and they touched the heart. And not only in their songs alone, but they seemed to spend all their lives in perpetual praise of one another. It seemed to be a universal and all-embracing love for each other. Some of their songs were solemn and ecstatic, and I was scarcely able to understand them at all. While understanding the words, I could never entirely fathom their meaning. It remained somehow beyond the grasp of my reason, and yet it sank unconsciously deeper and deeper into my heart. I often told them that I had had a presentiment of it years ago and that all that joy and glory had been perceived by me while

I was still on our earth as a nostalgic yearning, bordering at times on unendurably poignant sorrow; that I had had a presentiment of them all and of their glory in the dreams of my heart and in the reveries of my soul; that often on our earth I could not look at the setting sun without tears. . . . That there always was a sharp pang of anguish in my hatred of the men of our earth; why could I not hate them without loving them too? why could I not forgive them? And in my love for them, too, there was a sharp pang of anguish: why could I not love them without hating them? They listened to me, and I could tell that they did not know what I was talking about. But I was not sorry to have spoken to them of it, for I knew that they appreciated how much and how anxiously I yearned for those I had forsaken. Oh yes, when they looked at me with their dear eyes full of love, when I realised that in their presence my heart, too, became as innocent and truthful as theirs, I did not regret my inability to understand them, either. The sensation of the fullness of life left me breathless, and I worshipped them in silence.

Oh, everyone laughs in my face now and everyone assures me that I could not possibly have seen and felt anything so definite, but was merely conscious of a sensation that arose in my own feverish heart, and that I invented all those details myself when I woke up. And when I told them that they were probably right, good Lord, what mirth that admission of mine caused and how they laughed at me! Why, of course, I was overpowered by the mere sensation of that dream and it alone survived in my sorely wounded heart. But none the less the real shapes and forms of my dream, that is, those I actually saw at the very time of my dream, were filled with such harthe Fall was I. Like a horrible trichina, like the germ of the plague infecting whole kingdoms, so did I infect with myself all that happy earth that knew no sin before me. They learnt to lie, and they grew to appreciate the beauty of a lie. Oh, perhaps, it all began *innocently*, with a jest, with a desire to show off, with amorous play, and perhaps indeed only with a germ, but this germ made its way into their hearts and they liked it. The voluptuousness was soon born, voluptuousness begot jealousy, and jealousy—cruelty. . . . Oh, I don't know, I can't remember, but soon, very soon the first blood was shed; they were shocked and horrified, and they began to separate and to shun one another. They formed alliances, but it was one against another. Recriminations began, reproaches. They came to know shame, and they made shame into a virtue. The conception of honour was born, and every alliance raised its own standard. They began torturing animals, and the animals ran away from them into the forests and became their enemies. A struggle began for separation, for isolation, for personality, for mine and thine. They began talking in different languages. They came to know sorrow, and they loved sorrow. They thirsted for suffering, and they said that Truth could only be attained through suffering. It was then that science made its appearance among them. When they became wicked, they began talking of brotherhood and humanity and understood the meaning of those ideas. When they became guilty of crimes, they invented justice, and drew up whole codes of law, and to ensure the carrying out of their laws they erected a guillotine. They only vaguely remembered what they had lost, and they would not believe that they ever were happy and innocent. They even laughed at the possibility of their former happiness and called it a dream. They could not even imagine it in any definite shape or form, but the strange and wonderful thing was that though they had lost faith in their former state of happiness and called it a fairy-tale, they longed so much to be happy and innocent once more that, like children, they succumbed to the desire of their hearts, glorified this desire, built temples, and began offering up prayers to their own idea, their own "desire," and at the same time firmly believed that it could not be realised and brought about, though they still worshipped it and adored it with tears. And yet if they could have in one way or another returned to the state of happy innocence they had lost, and if someone had shown it to them again and had asked them whether they desired to go back to it, they would certainly have refused. The answer they gave me was, "What if we are dishonest, cruel, and unjust? We *know* it and we are sorry for it, and we torment ourselves for it, and inflict pain upon ourselves, and punish ourselves more perhaps than the merciful Judge who will judge us and whose name we do not know. But we have science and with its aid we shall again discover truth, though we shall accept it only when we perceive it with our reason. Knowledge is higher than feeling, and the consciousness of life is higher than life. Science will give us wisdom. Wisdom will reveal to us the laws. And the knowledge of the laws of happiness is higher than happiness." That is what they said to me, and having uttered those words, each of them began to love himself better than anyone else, and indeed they could not do otherwise. Every one of them became so jealous of his own personality that he strove with might and main to belittle and humble it in others; and therein he saw the whole purpose of his life. Slavery made its among them, wringing my hands and weeping over them, but I loved them perhaps more than before when there was no sign of suffering in their faces and when they were innocent and—oh, so beautiful! I loved the earth they had polluted even more than when it had been a paradise, and only because sorrow had made its appearance on it. Alas, I always loved sorrow and affliction, but only for myself, only for myself; for them I wept now, for I pitied them. I stretched out my hands to them, accusing, cursing, and despising myself. I told them that I alone was responsible for it all—I alone; that it was I who had brought them corruption, contamination, and lies! I implored them to crucify me, and I taught them how to make the cross. I could not kill myself; I had not the courage to do it; but I longed to receive martyrdom at their hands. I thirsted for martyrdom, I yearned for my blood to be shed to the last drop in torment and suffering. But they only laughed at me, and in the end they began looking upon me as a madman. They justified me. They said that they had got what they themselves wanted and that what was now could not have been otherwise. At last they told me that I was becoming dangerous to them and that they would lock me up in a lunatic asylum if I did not hold my peace. Then sorrow entered my soul with such force that my heart was wrung and I felt as though I were dying, and then—well, then I awoke.

It was morning, that is, the sun had not risen yet, but it was about six o'clock. When I came to, I found myself in the same armchair, my candle had burnt out, in the captain's room they were asleep, and silence, so rare in our house, reigned around. The first thing I did was to jump up in great amazement. Nothing like this had ever happened to me before, not even so far as the most trivial details were concerned. Never, for instance, had I fallen asleep like this in my armchair. Then, suddenly, as I was standing and coming to myself, I caught sight of my gun lying there ready and loaded. But I pushed it away from me at once! Oh, how I longed for life, life! I lifted up my hands and called upon eternal Truth—no, not called upon it, but wept. Rapture, infinite and boundless rapture intoxicated me. Yes, life and—preaching! I made up my mind to preach from that very moment and, of course, to go on preaching all my life. I am going to preach, I want to preach. What? Why, truth. For I have beheld truth, I have beheld it with mine own eyes, I have beheld it in all its glory!

And since then I have been preaching. Moreover, I love all who laugh at me more than all the rest. Why that is so, I don't know and I cannot explain, but let it be so. They say that even now I often get muddled and confused and that if I am getting muddled and confused now, what will be later on? It is perfectly true. I do get muddled and confused and it is quite possible that I shall be getting worse later. And, of course, I shall get muddled several times before I find out how to preach, that is, what words to use and what deeds to perform, for that is all very difficult! All this is even now as clear to me as daylight, but, pray, tell me who does not get muddled and confused? And yet all follow the same path, at least all strive to achieve the same thing, from the philosopher to the lowest criminal, only by different roads. It is an old truth, but this is what is new: I cannot even get very much muddled and confused. For I have beheld the Truth. I have beheld it and I know that people can be happy and beautiful without losing their ability to live on earth. I will not and I cannot believe that evil is the normal condition among men. And yet they all laugh at this faith of mine. But how can I help believing it? I have beheld it—the Truth—it is not as though I had invented it with my mind: I have beheld it, I have beheld it, and the *living image* of it has filled my soul for ever. I have beheld it in all its glory and I cannot believe that it cannot exist among men. So how can I grow muddled and confused? I shall of course lose my way and I'm afraid that now and again I may speak with words that are not my own, but not for long: the living image of what I beheld will always be with me and it will always correct me and lead me back on to the right path. Oh, I'm in fine fettle, and I am of good cheer. I will go on and on for a thousand years, if need be. Do you know, at first I did not mean to tell you that I corrupted them, but that was a mistake—there you have my first mistake! But Truth whispered to me that I was *lying*, and so preserved me and set me on the right path. But I'm afraid I do not know how to establish a heaven on earth, for I do not know how to put it into words. After my dream I lost the knack of putting things into words. At least, onto the most necessary and most important words. But never mind, I shall go on and I shall keep on talking, for I have indeed beheld it with my own eyes, though I cannot describe what I saw. It is this the scoffers do not understand. "He had a dream," they say, "a vision, a hallucination!" Oh dear, is this all they have to say? Do they really think that is very clever? And how proud they are! A dream! What is a dream? And what about our life? Is that not a dream too? I will say more: even—yes, even if this never comes to pass, even if there never is a heaven on earth (that, at any rate, I can see very well!), even then I shall go on preaching. And really how simple it all is: in one day, *in one hour*,

AN EXTRA STORY

ST. LUIS OF PALMYRA

FROM *MORE OF THIS WORLD OR MAYBE ANOTHER*
BY BARB JOHNSON

AVAILABLE FROM HARPER PERENNIAL
IN NOVEMBER 2009

Luis eases down the hall to where his mama's door is still closed. She's been crashed in her room since he got home from school. The Krewe of Idiots—that's what Luis calls Junior and his friends—is laid out all around the living room. Junior Palacios is his mama's boyfriend, and he doesn't go anywhere without the Idiots, a group of grown men whose only job in life is to follow Junior around and do whatever he says.

In the hallway, Luis stretches up on tiptoe, watches the living room through a fist-sized hole in the hall door. The Idiots are running their mouths about what all they're fixing to do. Big talk about whose car might be just about to disappear and who shouldn't sit on his porch unless he's looking to take the big nap. What they actually do is, the skinny ones fire up some meth and the fat ones smoke a joint. And then everybody's like:

Put it on *America's Most Wanted*! And: Gimme the remote, boy! And: Boy? Boy? Go home and tell your mama you got beat up by a boy! All the yelling cracks Luis up. It seems like everyone would know by now that the remote has to sit on top of Junior's big fat stomach. If you want to watch TV, you're gonna watch what Junior wants to watch. Why argue? But the Idiots always do. That's what makes them Idiots.

"Deysi, you can get your own ass up," Junior yells to Luis's mama, "or I can come in there and get it up for you. You been home all day and we got jack to eat!"

Luis could point out that Junior ain't been about much today either, but when he gets in the middle of that kind of stuff, it just makes it worse for his mama, so he usually keeps his mouth shut, goes outside until whatever's coming has been and gone. Sometimes Junior passes out without having to hit anybody.

Luis opens the hall door, keeps his eyes on his own feet. He scoots along the back edge of the living room, into the kitchen, then out the back door. Junior and the Idiots are like dogs or like those giant flying cockroaches: If you make eye contact with them, they feel like they've got to come after you. Luis doesn't have time for all that mess.

Tomorrow is the sixth grade science fair, and Luis is pretty sure he's gonna win it because science is his best subject. Science doesn't care how big you are; anyone can make it work, which is good for Luis, who's the smallest kid in his grade. He's gonna do a project that shows what makes a radio run. All he needs is a few parts, and he knows just the place to get them.

Luis karate-kicks his way down the alley next to the house. Hi-yah! He's ready to knock the nuts off of anybody hiding there in the dark. When he gets to the back pier of the house, he reaches under and runs his fingers along the sill until he snags his screwdriver, the good one he found outside Spanky's Automotive. It's got "Lifetime Guarantee" stamped right into the handle.

Somebody dumped a red BMW a little farther down Palmyra Street, across from the Laundromat. Luis has been hanging out in it at night. Making plans. He might take that car straight to MTV. Take his mama with him and maybe a dog, like a pit bull, the kind with those spooky blue eyes. Then if somebody looked at him wrong, Luis wouldn't say a thing. Wouldn't have to say, Mess with me, and my dog gonna fuck you up. He'd let that bad boy's teeth do all the talking.

Just before he gets to his car, Luis sees Miss Delia, who owns The Bubble, which is what everyone calls the Laundromat. She's standing up against the wall by the old pay phone. He watches her take a hit off her cigarette, tip her head back, and one-two-three-four smoke rings come floating out of her mouth.

It seems like to Luis that if you own a place, you should be able to do whatever you want. When Miss Delia wants to smoke at The Bubble, though, she has to do it on the side of the building that doesn't have any windows because she's supposed to be quitting. Miss Maggie, the other Laundromat lady, gets ten dollars every time she catches Miss Delia with a cigarette. Luis wishes Miss Delia would make that same deal with him. He holds up ten fingers to show her she's been caught. Miss Delia puts the cigarette behind her back and rocks her finger at Luis to say, Nuh-uh. Don't tell.

"You got homework at the library again?" Miss Delia calls across to Luis.

That's a joke they have. Luis's teacher's too lazy to give homework or check it, either one. Whenever Miss Delia asks him what he's up to in the car, though, Luis likes to tell her he's doing homework.

"I'm working on my science project," Luis says, and it sounds just right. Like he could do a project and win the science fair tomorrow, no problem. He points to the BMW. "I'm gonna . . ." Before he gets to the end of the sentence Luis realizes that he can't tell her about the radio project. If she knows he's gonna take the radio from the BMW, she might want to tell him it's wrong. Then she'll watch him to make sure he doesn't take it. And she for sure won't aim her scar at it for him. Taking the radio isn't wrong. It's just the way it is. "I got a secret, super-sonic, stealth-bomber project," he says, "and those punks are gonna be sorry they ever thought about trying to be in the science fair with me."

The second he's in the car, Luis sees that the radio, which for sure was there two nights ago, is gone, just gone. He checks the back floorboard where he's been stashing his schoolbooks. Nobody's touched them. Figures. No way he's gonna win the science fair now. Probably somebody's gonna make a poster or some rock candy and win. Which is how the world is. The same losers win everything because the good stuff gets jacked before you can get to it.

Luis reaches under the driver's seat for his new catechism book. Still there. When he told his mama he needed a new book, she just wanted to talk about how money don't grow on trees. Everybody knows money don't grow on trees. Luis wonders why people go on and ask you if you think it does. It gets on his nerves. "Ask Junior for the money," his mama told him, but Luis isn't about asking Junior for anything.

He could've bought a new book with his own money, but he's been saving up for in case he gets confirmed next week. Father Ben said don't count on it. But he also said Luis might be able to pass if he turned in the rest of his assignments. Luis felt like asking Father Ben how he was supposed to turn in his assignments if his book was lost. Priests don't understand regular things, though, so Luis just went on and got a new book off a girl in his class. She doesn't really need a book. She's got her some big old glasses, and they're thick. No way you could read a book through those coke bottles. Besides, girls get confirmed automatically because they're good.

Luis wants to tell Miss Delia about how he might be getting confirmed in case maybe she'll come to the party. People pin money on you at your Confirmation party, and probably Miss Delia's got a lot of it. But maybe not paper money. Sometimes Luis helps her count quarters out of a big bucket in the back room of The Bubble. Maybe she would bring that bucket to his party. She also has this shiny scar on her forehead, and she can aim at things and make them work right, like broken washing machines and wrong-acting children. Luis wonders if maybe she would use it to bring him good luck for the Confirmation party.

Junior says Confirmation is for suckers, and no way is God gonna let a little liar like Luis get confirmed. He told him flat out no when Luis had mentioned that maybe there should be a party for his Confirmation. He said, Oh no, Louise—Luis hates it when Junior calls him that—we ain't havin all those *cholos* over here. Luis hadn't even been talking to Junior at the time. He'd been talking to his mama, trying to get her to call his abuelita and tell her about the party because his grandmother knows how to get things done.

Abuelita is even smaller than Luis, but she's no saint. She will kick your ass if you cross her, and she's not scared of Junior like Luis's mama is. Which is why she's not invited to the house on Palmyra Street. Luis has to visit her at Hosea House, the old people's home a few blocks away, and that's probably for the best. Whenever Abuelita and Junior get around each other, it's never quiet for long.

The day Luis asked his mama about the party, she just shrugged her shoulders like she does for everything. She won't go against Junior. That's all right. When Luis gets confirmed, he'll be a man. He and his mama can leave Junior's ass, get in the BMW and go, and God can send Junior whatever he's got coming.

Luis sits up straight in the front seat of the car, stretches himself so he can hang his elbow out the window, then gives the steering wheel some serious attention. *Lookin good.* His feet don't touch the pedals when he sits like this, and Luis worries that he will never be taller than his mama, who is a girl after all. When he flips the visor down, a pair of sunglasses falls into his lap, and he puts them on in the dark car. *Smooth.* Occasionally Luis goes through Junior's pockets and takes things. Sometimes money, which Junior accused him of doing way before Luis actually started doing it, and sometimes things Luis knows will drive Junior crazy. His sunglasses, for example. Junior can't keep track of things like that, like sunglasses. But money? Well, Luis has several shiny pink scars on his head where hair should grow but won't.

If Junior's gonna hit him whether he's done anything or not, Luis figures he might as well take a little payment for it.

He crawls over to the back seat and puts on his miner's light so he can see. Father Ben said if Luis misses this last assignment, he'll for sure get left back and have to get confirmed with the babies in the class behind him. He says there won't be any cheating either, because cheating is a sin, and God won't stand for any sinning. Luis thinks God needs to make up His damn mind. If cheating is a sin and God loves even sinners, then God loves cheaters, which just goes to show how easy it is to get over on God. Luis guesses if it was just God standing between him and his Confirmation, no problem, but Father Ben don't play.

Write about the saint you most admire, the assignment sheet says. Luis digs around for some paper and finds the math worksheet he was looking for a while back. He erases the numbers, then taps the paper with his pencil for a while to make his thoughts come out. Father Ben likes ink, but that's because Father Ben has a nice fountain pen, and there ain't nobody at the rectory trying to get it away from him.

It takes Luis a couple of hours, but, when he's finished, there aren't any scratch-outs or misspelled words. There's not one thing Father Ben can say against it.

Saint Luis of Palmyra

The saint I admire is call Saint Luis of Palmyra. Saint Luis live way along time ago. Like before television. The reason I admire him is because he is a good guitar player. And he dont take no lip. Also because he is not like those other crazy kinda saints always boo-hoo somebody kilt me for loving Jesus. Even though Saint Luis love Jesus, he just dont talk about it all the time. He keep his stuff private. He just like make music and do some good deeds like if a old lady need to cross the street or something. Also he built that place MTV where everbody can go and just play music or videos and be on tv. This place is like Heaven and everbody look tight and can play music. Like all kinda music. Saint Luis is a good saint because if somebody hurt him, like a giant, he dont just stand there and ax for more. He would make a plan and smite that giant. He will help himself and his family and not wait around and see if the bad people are stop being bad. Or if Jesus gonna make a miracle out of it. The end.

Luis folds the essay just the way Father Ben likes it and slips it into his catechism book. He kicks back in the seat and puts his feet up in the open window, imagines himself at his Confirmation party in a new suit. All his relatives are there. His jacket is covered in money, and there's Miss Delia with a whole bucket of quarters. Luis hasn't mentioned the party around Junior again because Junior will only let the Krewe of Idiots come to the house. Luis is sure he can get Abuelita to make a party for him, and his other relatives will come if she's there.

Around midnight Luis jerks awake in the back seat when a car drives by, slow, music thumping. He quick rolls to the floorboard in case there's gonna be shooting. After the car passes, he looks out in the street. No one. The Bubble is dark except for the snack machine. It glows like a nightlight for Palmyra Street.

Luis meant to go across before Miss Delia left. After she closes at night, she unlocks that snack machine to put the new stuff in and take the money out, and sometimes she lets Luis pick something to eat or keep some quarters if he helps her put the change in those little paper wrappers.

He gets his catechism book and crosses to look at the snack machine through The Bubble's big window. 3C: animal cookies, his favorite. If you keep the elephant heads, you can make a wish and toss them over your left shoulder for good luck. If he'd been awake before Miss Delia left, he could've got a whole handful of elephant heads and then maybe he would've found a radio on the way home, like one nobody was using.

When he gets back to his house, it's dark except for the TV light. Luis was hoping Junior would already be passed out, but he's still on the couch, which is Luis's bed. The Idiots are slouched and slumped all around the living room, all of them snoring like it's a contest. One Idiot, the skinny one called Pudge, is laid out in the bathroom doorway like he's been murdered. He's got a big wet spot on the front of his pants that makes Luis want to kick him.

Junior's watching a fight on TV. Got a bottle of Wild Turkey parked on the coffee table, a glass of it wedged between his nuts. Luis hates that, how Junior puts everything where he has to touch his nuts to get at it.

Luis can tell that Junior's been waiting for him. If he doesn't give that fat *cabrón* what he wants, he'll just go after Luis's mama, and that's always some hitting. It's better just to do the deal and get it over with. Junior usually falls straight to sleep after, and then everybody can get some rest.

Luis puts his catechism book on the upside-down milk crate by the front door. He's mad about the science project. He should've checked some other cars. Like earlier in the week. Then he could've done that radio thing, no problem. But winning the science fair is for little kids anyway. The prize is just like a ribbon, and they say your name on the intercom at school. Big deal. Passing catechism and getting rid of Junior will be ten times as good as some candy-ass blue ribbon.

Junior's scratching his nuts, following Luis with his eyes. His head jerks on its neck like a sprinkler that can only turn a little at a time. What a moron. He probably couldn't make a science project or pass catechism, either one. Luis tries to picture Junior in a suit and tie or hooking up a radio at the science fair. What a joke.

"What you laughin at, *hijo*?" Junior asks, looking Luis right in the eye.

"Nothin."

"Well, either I'm crazy or you're lyin because I just saw you laugh. You see somethin here you think's funny?" Junior fingers the glass between his legs and runs his thumb up his dick. He makes that face at Luis, the one that says come on and don't make any noise.

"No sir. It ain't nothin funny." Luis kneels between Junior's legs, thinks about the bottle on the coffee table. In his mind, he picks it up and smacks Junior over the head, then slits his throat with the jagged broken edge.

Luis is late for school the next morning, and when he walks in, Mrs. Green—Luis calls her the Jolly Green Giant because she's like ten feet tall and got some bad breath on her—says, Boy, you don't get your shit together, there ain't gonna be no junior high for Luis Hernandez. Teachers always say that kind of thing to him, but he hasn't failed one time yet. The Giant says his name like LEW-iss, even though he's told her that's not how it's pronounced. She's too lazy to say a Spanish word, though.

The Giant tries to make science class boring with all her bullshit. She just wants to hang a string in a glass of sugar water and then you got rock candy. Candy is for babies. They've been doing that same experiment since like third grade. Luis wants to do the ones about sound waves, but you need some of those tuning fork things, and that would mean the Giant would have to get off her ass and go find some. No way that's gonna happen. In the book, though, it says if you hit that C fork, then you could hold it next to another C fork, and that one'll start making the C note, too. Without anyone even touching it. It's because they're the same. Things that are the same vibrate when they get next to each other.

All those experiments are way in the back of the book, though. They'll never get to them by the end of the year. They have science three days a week, and that's playtime for the Giant. Time to get that nail polish out.

The science fair is after lunch. Luis eats with his class, but when they go out for recess, he just keeps walking until he's out the gate. He pinched a sandwich for his mama off a girl's plate in the cafeteria. Not the screaming kind of girl, the quiet kind that will just cry but not tell. Grilled cheese is his mama's favorite.

When Luis gets to his house, he stands outside the kitchen door, listening. Quiet can be good. Or it can be trouble.

When he gets to his mama's bedroom, she and Junior are asleep on their sides, facing the open doorway, Junior with his pig arm pinning his mama. She's got a brand new cast that starts right above her knuckles and goes all the way up under her armpit. Luis wouldn't mind poking one of those tuning forks in Junior's eye. Hit another one and make that thing vibrate in his head. Long as you had a tuning fork, that fat *cabrón* couldn't come near you.

Luis decides he's gonna get his mama something nice, like a present. He looks around for Junior's pants. Before he can take a step, though, his mama opens her eyes. Looks right at him. Says don't do it with just a look. It's a scared look, and it vibrates in Luis.

Later that afternoon, after Junior goes to do a little business with the Idiots at the vacant house down the street, Luis sits with his mama. "I won the science fair," he tells her. "They said my name on the intercom. And then the mayor came. He said if we move to MTV, they got an apartment there for us. Free."

Luis's mama stares out the window like she can't hear him.

"I can stay with you instead of going to catechism," he tells her.

His mama reaches her hand out toward him. "Give me a couple of those." She points to a bottle of Vicodin on the nightstand. When he hands her the pills, she flips them into her mouth, chews them up. Almost right away, she's asleep again.

Catechism is clear across Mid-City at Our Lady of Prompt Succor. Luis has to weave through a bunch of second graders who are walking home from school. The little knuckleheads keep stopping to look at Luis can't tell what. Invisible stuff on the sidewalk or in the air or way up their noses. Then: Bam! They all take off running for the corner where two girls are in a fight. There's one left behind, a chubby little boy. He's got a great big cuff turned up on the bottom of his navy blue pants in case he ever gets tall enough to match up with how wide he is. And the kid's wearing the whitest shirt Luis has ever seen. It won't be white for long, though. *Gordo*'s got a bag of cheese puffs, and Luis knows he needs to make his move. a clean shirt will impress Father Ben, who unlike God has the power to keep Luis from making his Confirmation.

Luis does a fast walk, gets in front of the kid, then ducks into an alley.

"Hey kid," he says when the fat boy walks past.

The boy stops and looks down the alley, his hand moving like a piston, up-down, up-down, from the bag of Cheetos to his mouth. When he sees Luis, he tries to put the bag behind his back, but his fat little arms won't reach.

"I don't want your food, man. I need your help."

"My help?"

"Yeah, I need to borrow your shirt for just a minute."

Luis's shirt is the color of mop water next to this kid's, and he drops it right there in the alley then unbuttons the other boy's shirt. The kid starts crying. Luis can feel *gordo* shaking like a fat-boy tuning fork as he removes the clean white shirt from the kid's roly-poly back. Luis looks away in case the boy's eyes are gonna say don't, in case all that shaking is gonna make him shake, too. Luis imagines that God must be testing him with all these bad feelings. When he gets confirmed, when he's a man in God's sight, then God will realize that Luis did all of this for Jesus, who is love, and maybe He will stop giving him bad feelings.

"All right, now," Luis says, turning toward the street. "You wait here. I'll be right back."

The kid says okay, but in a whisper, like it's a secret. Little kids are so stupid. It's like somebody gave them drugs the way they'll just believe anything.

When Luis's classmates are dismissed to go to confession in church, Father Ben, who's still at his desk filling out Confirmation certificates, tells Luis to hold on just a second. He's got Luis's essay in his hand. "What's this?"

"That's my essay," Luis tells him.

"I know it's your essay, but who was St. Luis of Palmyra? I've never heard of him."

"It's all in there about who he was."

"Well, Luis, why do you think I've never heard of him even though I've been a priest for fifteen years?" Father Ben rolls up the essay into a tube and pops Luis on the head with it, but in a friendly way, not a mean way. Like he just told Luis a joke.

Luis explains to the priest that St. Luis was a new kind of saint they just found out about, even though he lived way a long time ago. St. Luis knew how to handle his business and wouldn't let his whole family get hacked up by some stupid giant. "Saints can't be so lazy anmore," Luis tells Father Ben. "They gotta deal." He points out that all the good people who became the old kind of saints got their heads busted open and then went straight up to Heaven, and that left all the head-busters down on Earth.

"Well, yeah," Father Ben says, "I can see how that would be a problem after a while."

Then Father Ben says *but* and stops like he's thinking, so Luis has to stand there and wait to hear what kind of mess is gonna be on the other side of that *but*. Any time somebody says something good and then says *but*, it's bad news.

When he can't wait any longer, Luis asks, "But what?"

Father Ben opens and closes his mouth, but no words come out. He unrolls the essay and reads down the whole page. "But nothing," he says finally. Luis waits for more, for the part where the priest is gonna say the essay isn't good enough and Luis should try again next year. When Father Ben puts out his hand, Luis is so shocked he just about leaves the priest hanging, but right before it's too late, he shakes it like a full-grown man.

Father Ben smiles at Luis. "Congratulations, my friend. You handled your business, and you passed catechism." Then Father Ben reminds Luis that the bishop will slap him during the Confirmation ceremony Sunday, but he shouldn't hit back. The slap is to remind Luis that he should be ready to suffer, even to die for what is right.

Luis wonders which *right* Father Ben is talking about. It looks like to Luis that nobody's ever talking about the same one.

"When you get confirmed, Luis," Father Ben adds, "it means that God is on your side, and having God on your side will give you the strength of a thousand men and the Wisdom of Solomon."

Luis isn't sure what that last part means, but it all sounds good. He closes his eyes and pictures the bishop slapping him.

In his mind he doesn't hit back. He can do it; he's sure of it.

Father Ben pulls out a certificate with Luis's name on it and uncaps the fountain pen that Luis once used to strafe a classmate. Ack-ack-ack-ack! The pen gun left blue blood splatters on the other boy's shirt. *All units in the vicinity, we got a 189 at Prep Succor.*

"Have you decided on a Confirmation name?" Father Ben asks.

Luis forgot about this part, about how you have to pick a saint's name to be your Confirmation name, and he lost the list that Father Ben gave everyone a long time ago. He wonders if this is a final test. If he guesses wrong, will Father Ben still pass him? The saint is supposed to protect you, and you're supposed to pick someone you want to be like. "Goliath?" Luis says. Goliath, a name like a pit bull.

"Goliath wasn't a saint, Luis. He was the mean giant who hurt everyone, remember?"

Of course Luis remembers, and he wonders again why all the saints have to be such sissies, why they can't be badasses worth looking up to. Although. It was David who kicked Goliath's ass, even though he was small like Luis, plus he could play one of those old-timey guitars. "Oh, I meant David," Luis says.

"David? Okay. David it is, then."

Luis watches "David" appear on the page, the straight backs of the two "d's" like the place you could attach rubber bands and make a slingshot to kill a giant. After the certificate is all filled out, Luis gets in line at the confessional with the other kids. Even though it's just Father Ben in there, Luis worries about what kind of sins to tell, what kind of sins a man has to confess. Finally he decides to say a little about some stealing, but he doesn't mention any names. He wonders if giving Junior a blow job is a sin if he's doing it to keep Junior off his mama. That's between him and God, Luis decides, and he confesses losing his temper instead. Father Ben gives him five Our Fathers and five Hail Marys as a penance, which is what he gives everyone no matter what they did.

After he's through with his penance, Luis kneels in the pew for a while studying the stained glass where the sun has turned into a spotlight over Jesus's head. It makes Jesus look like he just got a bright idea. That's what Luis needs, an idea about how to keep Junior away from his Confirmation party. Luis could use smiting, maybe. Everybody in the Bible smites their enemies, but usually God will smite them for you if He's on your side.

It doesn't seem right to expect God to do his work for him, but Luis isn't big enough to smite Junior himself or vex him either, which is another thing God does if you go against Him. Luis decides to ask God for an idea about what to do. But just an idea, because a man handles his business. He's pretty sure that if he can get a good idea of what to do, then he can do it himself because ideas are like science. You don't have to be big to use them. And the best kind of idea would be a science idea because science is what makes a song come out of a radio. Or a tuning fork vibrate without touching it. Luis bets it can make a fat *cabrón* miss a party, too.

The night before his Confirmation, Luis is in the backseat of the BMW, waiting for Miss Delia to close up The Bubble across the street. While he waits, he practices his prayers for the ceremony.

He's timed it, and he can say the Act of Contrition in fifteen seconds flat, no peeking at the book. He's ready.

This afternoon, Abuelita sent Luis home with three huge platters of food that she and her friends cooked after hours, right there in the Hosea House kitchen. When Luis brought the food in, Junior told him that he better not be planning to invite any relatives over after Confirmation, and Luis said no way, which is the truth. It was Abuelita who called everyone.

Luis has to fast now, which means he can't eat anything until his party tomorrow to show that he's willing to suffer for God. As of midnight, he'll be a man, and God will be on his side. He knows his prayers. He's got a suit, and he's got a fistful of sleepy-time for Junior. Thirty-six Vicodin he took out of the big bottle by his mama's bed. The label on the bottle said one every six hours, which is four a day, but Junior's huge, and it takes a lot to stop him from doing what he wants to do. Luis figures he's only gonna have one shot at getting Junior out of the way, so he's gonna give him all thirty-six at once. Enough to make him sleep through the party and maybe a couple of extra days. That way Luis will have time to get the BMW going, and he and his mama can drive off, maybe get to MTV, but for sure be long gone before Junior wakes up.

Across the street, Luis watches Miss Delia lock The Bubble up. "See you tomorrow!" she says, giving Luis a wave and riding off on her bike. Once she's out of sight, Luis reaches under the front seat and pulls out a bottle of Bailey's Irish Cream, borrowed from Abuelita's. It's the most important ingredient for the party tomorrow. Pushing open the car door, he drains most of the bottle into the gutter, leaving just enough to fill Junior's special drink glass.

Luis unties a camouflage bandana with a jawbreaker-sized knot of Vicodin powder in it. Yesterday in science class, while the Giant was getting her nails done, Luis used his compass and a ruler to smash all the pills into tiny bits on the bandana. He twisted that pile of powder into a knot and tied it around his neck. Since then, that knot's been beating with the pulse in his throat: Joon-yer, Joon-yer, Joon-yer. Luis drops the powder a pinch at a time into the bottle. After each pinch, he heats the liquid with a lighter—an old silver one that Junior stole off one of the Idiots— then shakes the bottle, hard, until all the pills are dissolved in the milky drink. He's read in his science book that when a solid completely dissolves in a liquid, it becomes a solution.

When Luis walks through the front door just after midnight, Junior is still awake. *COPS* is on the TV. A guy with a bleeding head, who's wearing nothing but a pair of ladies' drawers, is face down in the street surrounded by the police. It's over for him.

From the plate on his lap, Junior is tossing *flautas* into his mouth. Bing, bang, boom, that *cabrón* is wrecking the neat pyramid that Abuelita made with the food. He looks over at Luis, his eyes all googly and red. "Whatchu got there, *hijo*?" he asks when he catches sight of the bottle Luis is carrying.

"Nothin."

"Look like some expensive nothin to me. Whatchu doin with that?" Junior digs under the platter of food, pulls his glass from between his legs.

"Abuelita said it's a Confirmation present for my mama," Luis answers, already thinking of his party, his new suit, Abuelita grilling the chicken he hid in the vegetable drawer.

"Look like you already had you some."

"No sir. She just sent this little bit."

"Fuckin *cholos*," Junior says, his head bobbing like a balloon on his neck. "Better give me that, then, and don't say nothin to your mama." Junior motions for Luis to open the bottle, shoves his glass out to be filled.

"No sir," Luis says, emptying the bottle into the glass, "I won't say a thing." He goes over and stands next to the door and watches Junior kill the drink in a few greedy gulps, then Luis drags the milk crate over to a place where he can see the TV.

"Loser!" Junior yells at the guy on *COPS* who's hiding under a plastic swimming pool. The two cops who've been chasing him shake their heads at the half-assed job the junkie's done. His foot is sticking out right where they're standing.

By the time the credits roll on the second of the back-to-back episodes, Junior's face has tipped up toward the ceiling, and he's snorting and snoring. Luis goes over and takes the plate off his lap. He does his best to stack what's left of the *flautas* the way Abuelita had them, then takes them back to the refrigerator where they belong. He scrubs Junior's drink glass, runs hot water into it, then polishes it with a clean dish towel and puts it away in the cupboard.

Back in the living room, Luis grabs the remote off Junior's stomach. He flips through the channels until he comes to a show about how bridges get built. On the TV, a smart-looking man in khakis and glasses studies his plans, big blue drawings on a table he set up right at the edge of a cliff.

The water is so far down and so wide, it gives Luis the willies to think about it. Rocks poke out of the ground everywhere, and there must be snakes, too. For sure no place to stand when it comes time to start building. Luis can't imagine how anyone could make a way to get over all that mess. But sure enough, an hour into the program, the man with the glasses stands pointing across the completed bridge. Luis watches him get into a car, wave to the crowd, then drive to the other side.